*I would like to express my special thanks
to Catherine Hapka for her help
in the writing of this book.*

THE SADDLE CLUB

HORSE RACE

BONNIE BRYANT

A SKYLARK BOOK
NEW YORK • TORONTO • LONDON • SYDNEY • AUCKLAND

RL 5, 009–012

HORSE RACE

A Bantam Skylark Book / September 1997

Skylark Books is a registered trademark of Bantam Books, a division of Bantam Doubleday Dell Publishing Group, Inc. Registered in U.S. Patent and Trademark Office and elsewhere.

"The Saddle Club" is a registered trademark of Bonnie Bryant Hiller. The Saddle Club design/logo, which consists of a riding crop and a riding hat, is a trademark of Bantam Books.

"USPC" and "Pony Club" are registered trademarks of The United States Pony Clubs, Inc., at The Kentucky Horse Park, 4071 Iron Works Pike, Lexington, KY 40511-8462.

ISBN 0-553-48425-7

Published simultaneously in the United States and Canada.

Bantam Books are published by Bantam Books, a division of Bantam Doubleday Dell Publishing Group, Inc. Its trademark, consisting of the words "Bantam Books" and the portrayal of a rooster, is Registered in U.S. Patent and Trademark Office and in other countries. Marca Registrada. Bantam Books, 1540 Broadway, New York, New York 10036.

PRINTED IN THE UNITED STATES OF AMERICA

OPM   0 9 8 7 6 5 4 3 2 1

"HOW DOES IT GO?" Stevie Lake asked. "It's something about a horse with a funny name. George Washington? Winston Churchill?"

Her two best friends, Carole Hanson and Lisa Atwood, ignored her. They were busy watching the lush, beautiful landscape rolling past the car windows.

"Look at that," Carole said, sounding a little breathless.

Lisa didn't have to ask what she meant. She, too, had seen the white-fenced field of bright green grass they were passing. Several Thoroughbred mares were grazing near the fence while their foals frolicked nearby, chasing and nipping at one another playfully.

"I can't believe we're really in Kentucky." Lisa sighed happily.

The driver of the car, Deborah Hale, glanced over and

1

took in the sight. "Those are some big babies," she commented. Deborah was a newspaper reporter. She was married to Max Regnery, the owner of Pine Hollow Stables in Willow Creek, Virginia. Pine Hollow was where Stevie, Carole, and Lisa had met and become best friends. It was also where they had formed The Saddle Club, which had only two rules: Members had to be horse-crazy, and they had to be willing to help each other out whenever and however it was necessary.

"They *are* big," Carole agreed, turning to get a last glimpse of the foals as the car continued past the field. "Most of them are probably at least five months old. They'll be ready for weaning in a month or so." It was late August, and Carole knew that future racehorses were usually born early in the year and weaned sometime around October. Of the three horse-crazy girls, she was the horse-craziest. She liked to know everything there was to know about everything having to do with horses.

"Poor babies," Lisa said. "I always feel sorry for them when they cry for their mothers." Weaning was when a young horse was taken away from its mother and switched from mare's milk to more adult feed. The weanlings usually cried and complained for a few days before settling down.

By now Stevie had stopped humming and was leaning forward to look over Carole's shoulder at another field of mares and foals. All three girls were sitting in the backseat, which had made Deborah joke that she felt like a chauffeur.

"I know what you mean, Lisa," Stevie said. "But weaning *is* necessary." She grinned. "All those big, strong, fancy racehorses would look awfully funny heading out for the starting gate with their mommies trotting along next to them."

The others laughed at the image. "Well, I'm still glad that Maxi and I won't have to go through anything like that," Deborah joked. Maxi, short for Maxine, was her three-month-old daughter.

Lisa gave her a sympathetic look. "It must be hard leaving her behind for this trip, isn't it?"

"It *is* hard," Deborah agreed. "It's the first time I've been away for more than a few hours since she was born." She shrugged. "But Max will be home to take care of her, and my editor really wanted me to come out here to research this story. I've been trying so long to get more experience reporting at the track that I didn't want to turn her down." She sighed. "Even though I miss my daughter like crazy already."

Carole nodded understandingly. "I know what you mean. I miss Starlight already, too."

Her friends laughed, and Carole gave them a surprised look. Maybe most people wouldn't think that missing her horse could be compared to missing a new baby, but to Carole it made perfect sense. After all, Starlight was a very special horse.

Suddenly a strange look crossed Stevie's face and she sat up as straight as her seat belt would allow.

"I've got it!" she shouted. "Paul Revere."

Carole and Lisa turned to stare at her, and Deborah glanced in the rearview mirror.

"What?" Lisa asked for all of them.

Stevie grinned sheepishly. "Paul Revere," she said. "That's the name of the horse in the song I was trying to think of." She hummed a few bars. "It's from the musical *Guys and Dolls*. The whole song is about betting on horses. It's very funny."

"I've seen that," Carole said. "My dad loves the movie."

Lisa just rolled her eyes. "That's very interesting, Stevie," she said dryly. "But can't we end the sing-along for now? I, for one, am dying to hear more about the story Deborah's going to be researching while we're here." They had left home very early that morning, so the three girls had spent the first part of the trip sleeping. Then, when they woke up, they spent the next part of the ride talking about the wonderful summer they had just spent riding and having fun. That, of course, had reminded them that school would be starting in just a couple of weeks, and they had spent some time discussing that. Then Stevie had started trying to come up with racing-themed songs. The upshot was that in all the hours they had been traveling, The Saddle Club had hardly had time to talk about the reason for their trip. Deborah was going to a racetrack in Kentucky called Bluegrass Park to research her latest assignment, and she had invited The Saddle Club to come along with her.

Stevie quieted down, and Deborah nodded agreeably.

"Well, you all know it's a feature story on up-and-coming young trainers," she began.

"Right," Carole said. "And one of them works for Mr. McLeod, right?" David McLeod owned a racing stable not far from Willow Creek called Maskee Farms. The girls had gotten to know him and his beautiful Thoroughbreds during several previous visits. They had also taken a trip to Maryland to see one of his fastest horses, Monkeyshines, race in the famous Preakness Stakes.

"Right," Deborah confirmed. "You've all met Mr. McLeod's regular trainer, but this weekend I'm going to be interviewing his assistant trainer. His name is Garvey Cannon, and he's only been working at Maskee for a couple of months. But he's supposed to be awfully good. Mr. McLeod let him bring some of his most promising two-year-olds to Bluegrass while he and the head trainer are out in California."

Carole shook her head. "I still can't believe Thoroughbreds start racing when they're only two," she said. "That makes Starlight seem practically ancient, doesn't it?" Starlight had been only four years old when Carole first got him. And she had thought *that* was young!

"I guess it's a good thing Starlight's not a racehorse," Stevie joked. "Otherwise his career would probably be nearly over by now."

"Not necessarily," Lisa protested. "He might just be ready to start his *second* career." The others laughed. They knew Lisa was thinking about Prancer, the horse she usually rode at Pine Hollow. Prancer had been one of Mr. McLeod's racehorses, but a weak bone in her foot had ended her career on the track. Now she had a new career as a lesson horse.

Carole glanced out the window as they passed another field, where a lone horse gazed out over the fence at them. "It's too bad our friends won't be at the racetrack this time," she said. Then, realizing that she might sound ungrateful, she glanced at Deborah. "But this trip is going to be great anyway," she added quickly.

Deborah laughed. "Don't worry, I know what you mean," she said, turning the wheel a little to avoid a rock. "I'd like to see the old gang, too, especially Eddie and Stephen." Eddie was a Maskee groom, and Stephen was Mr. McLeod's usual jockey.

"I don't think that's who Carole was thinking of," Stevie put in with a grin. "The ones *she's* going to miss are Hold Fast and Monkeyshines."

The others laughed while Carole blushed. She *had* been thinking of the two horses when she had spoken. "I'll miss the people, too," she said defensively. That just made everyone laugh even harder.

"Anyway," Deborah said when the laughter had quieted down, "the usual gang—people *and* horses—are out at one of the California racetracks for some important stakes races. But Mr. McLeod didn't want his younger horses to miss their chance to run, *and* he didn't want to ship them all out to California, so he sent them to Kentucky with Garvey."

6

She shrugged. "That's lucky for me, since several of the other trainers I need to interview will be at Bluegrass Park this weekend, too."

"Why do they call Kentucky the Bluegrass State, anyway?" Stevie asked, looking out the window again. "The grass here all looks pretty green to me."

Carole rolled her eyes. "Don't change the subject, Stevie," she ordered. "We're talking about horses, not grass."

"I thought we were talking about trainers," Lisa said mischievously.

Deborah laughed. "Actually, I was just getting to the horses," she said. "Maskee has about half a dozen horses at Bluegrass right now, but there are a few very promising youngsters in the bunch. One in particular is a filly named Cookie Cutter."

"Oh, let me guess," Stevie said immediately. "Um, her mother's name is probably Dessert, right? And her sire must be Chocolate Chip. Or maybe Mixing Bowl."

The others giggled at the guesses. They knew that sometimes the owners of Thoroughbreds came up with names for their foals by combining both parents' names. "How do you know Cookie Cutter is named after her sire and dam?" Carole teased. "Maybe Mr. McLeod was just feeling a little hungry when he came up with the name."

"Actually, Cookie Cutter *is* named after her parents," Deborah said. "But your guesses are a bit off, Stevie. Her dam is Baker's Dozen, and her sire is Swordplay."

"Sword—Oh, I get it." Stevie grinned. "Cookie *Cutter*. That's clever."

But Carole was less interested in the horse's name than the horse herself. "Is Cookie Cutter as fast as Monkeyshines?" she asked.

"It's a little early to tell that," Deborah said. "In fact, it's a little early for anyone to be talking about Cookie Cutter at all, since her very first race is the day after tomorrow. It's unusual for an unraced horse to be so highly regarded. But her bloodlines are excellent, and she's shown a lot of speed in her workouts."

"You sound like an old pro talking about this stuff, Deborah," Carole said admiringly.

Deborah shrugged. "I know some of the lingo, but I'm still no pro," she said honestly. "I'm learning, though—as fast as I can." She paused, and a very interesting twinkle came into her eye as she glanced at the girls in the rearview mirror. Stevie noticed it and wondered what it meant. "For instance," Deborah continued, "did you know that there are people at the track whose only job is walking horses to cool them down after a workout?"

Carole nodded. She knew that from her previous visits to the racetrack. "They're called hot-walkers, right?"

"Right," Deborah said. She paused again. "Well, as soon as I heard that the Maskee barn was a little short-staffed because the regular people are out in California, I started thinking: Who do I know with experience walking horses who would be willing to pitch in and help out?"

Lisa gasped. "You mean . . . ?"

Deborah nodded, taking her eyes off the road just long enough to glance back at the girls again. This time all three of them saw the twinkle in her eyes. "I hope you don't mind," she said. "I volunteered you to be hot-walkers while we're here this weekend."

All three girls started talking at once, thrilled at the idea of helping care for Mr. McLeod's beautiful Thoroughbred racehorses. For a second nothing they said made much sense, but they knew Deborah wouldn't mind.

Stevie was the first to regain the power of coherent speech. "This is going to be great," she declared.

"I hope so," Deborah said, smiling. "It's going to be hard work, you know. Garvey has only two full-time grooms working with him this weekend, which makes them really short-staffed. He may need you to pitch in as unofficial assistant grooms, too." She paused again, and her smile grew broader. "I guess that's probably why Mr. McLeod insisted on paying you the going rate for hot-walkers."

"What?" Carole could hardly believe it. Mr. McLeod was actually going to pay them to do something they would gladly do for free? "He doesn't have to do that!"

"But he can if he wants to," Stevie put in quickly, shooting Carole a look. Stevie was famous for spending her allowance as quickly as she got it. She was always in need of extra cash.

"Actually, he insisted on it," Deborah said. "After all, if it weren't for you girls, he'd have to hire people locally to do the work. But before you get too excited, I'd better warn you that hot-walking is just about the most menial job there is at the track. It doesn't pay a lot."

But when she told them how much they'd be getting, Stevie let out a whistle. "That sounds pretty good to me," she said.

Lisa nodded. "It's more than I make baby-sitting," she admitted.

"And wouldn't you rather baby-sit horses than humans anyway?" Carole put in.

Deborah smiled at her in the rearview mirror. "Does that mean you'd rather muck out stalls than play with Maxi, Carole?" she teased.

Carole shrugged and grinned. "It's a toss-up," she teased right back. Then she leaned back in her seat and returned to watching the gorgeous Kentucky landscape rush by. "Money or no money, it was awfully nice of you to ask us along on this trip," she told Deborah.

"I can't take all the credit," Deborah admitted. "As soon as I mentioned the trip, Max suggested I take you with me." She laughed. "Actually, he sort of insisted. Then he mumbled something about back-to-school blues and moping girls . . ."

The Saddle Club exchanged glances. They *had* been awfully depressed about returning to school after such an exciting summer—even Lisa, who actually liked school most of the time.

"Poor Max," Lisa said. "We must have really been driving

him crazy if he went out of his way to send us on such a great trip. What are the odds of that?"

Deborah gave her a surprised look. " 'What are the odds of that?' " she repeated. "Where did you pick up that expression?" It wasn't a phrase Lisa used every day of the week.

Lisa grinned. "Hey, we *are* heading for the racetrack, right?"

"Who cares about the odds or why he did it?" Carole put in. "The important thing is that we're here. Right, Stevie?"

But Stevie wasn't paying attention. She was singing again. " 'Camptown ladies sing this song, doo-da, doo-da.' "

Carole rolled her eyes. "If you don't know the words, why bother to sing the song?"

But Lisa recognized the song from her piano lessons. "Those *are* the words, Carole," she said. She joined in to sing with Stevie for the next line: " 'Camptown racetrack five miles long, oh, doo-da day!' "

Before long, Carole and Deborah had picked up the tune and were singing along.

After a few minutes Carole noticed that the farms were getting smaller and the houses closer together. "We must be getting closer to town," she said, breaking up the sing-along.

Deborah nodded and stifled a yawn. "We're almost to our hotel," she said. "Thank goodness. I don't think I could drive much farther. I'm ready for a quick dinner and an early bedtime."

"Too bad," Carole said. "Because I could look at Kentucky for hours and hours more. It's beautiful."

11

"Maybe we'll have a chance to drive out and look around some more tomorrow or the next day," Deborah said. "I can't make any promises, though—my story is going to keep me awfully busy. And your work will keep you pretty busy, too." She smiled. "But I know you'll find some time to have fun. You always do, right?"

"Right," The Saddle Club answered in one voice.

LISA RUBBED HER EYES. Carole yawned. Stevie stretched her arms wearily.

"Are we really awake?" Lisa mumbled. It was five-thirty A.M., and they had just climbed out of Deborah's car near the stable area of Bluegrass Park.

"I'm not sure," Carole said. "I'm afraid it may be a dream, since Stevie isn't singing 'doo-da, doo-da.' " Stevie had kept the others up half the night by singing "Camptown Races" in her sleep.

"I told you girls you could sleep for another hour," Deborah said. "The exercise riders don't get here until about six, and the hot-walkers start after that." She sounded just as wide awake and cheerful as always. Lisa guessed that Deborah was used to getting by on minimum sleep because of the baby. Of course, not sharing a room with Stevie probably helped, too.

"We're not just hot-walkers," Carole said. "We're unofficial assistant grooms, too, right?" She stifled another yawn. "That means we've got to be here early."

"Have it your way," Deborah said, looking amused. "Come on, let's go meet everyone." She led the way through the maze of barns with the three tired girls stumbling after her.

Lisa woke up a little when she recognized the Maskee Farms colors decorating one of the shed rows. She followed as Deborah led them inside.

All three girls felt a lot more awake once they were inside the long, narrow stable. Outside the track gates, most people were still sleeping, but in here the day had already begun. Horses looked out of their stalls or munched on the last few bites of their breakfasts. Music was pouring out of a small portable radio plugged in at the far end of the row. A tall, athletic-looking bay colt was in cross-ties being carefully groomed by a young woman with a ponytail. Two men were deep in discussion just a few yards away.

"That's Garvey Cannon," Deborah whispered to The Saddle Club, nodding toward the taller of the pair. "I recognize him from his picture."

"You mean you've never met him?" Stevie asked.

Deborah shook her head. Then she stepped forward and introduced herself to the young trainer. Garvey was large and broad-shouldered, with a thick neck and huge arm muscles. Atop his bulk, his head, with its ruddy skin and thin blond hair, seemed almost too small. The assistant trainer looked even larger next to his companion, a tiny, slender man Lisa guessed was a jockey or exercise rider.

"So you're the reporter McLeod was talking about," Garvey said flatly as the small man wandered off toward the bay colt in the aisle. Lisa noticed that Garvey didn't smile. In fact, he didn't look very pleased to see Deborah at all.

Deborah nodded and gestured for the girls to step forward. "And these are your temporary hot-walkers," she said. She started to introduce them, but Garvey cut her off.

"Them?" he said in disbelief. "But they're just kids. These are valuable animals we've got here, you know, not hacking ponies."

Lisa felt her face flush at Garvey's tone. But once Deborah had reassured him that Mr. McLeod had approved the whole thing, Garvey seemed to relax a little. "Okay, he's the boss," he said with a shrug of his huge shoulders. He glanced at the three girls. "I just hope you know what you're doing," he added. "We've got some important races coming up this weekend. I don't want anything to hurt our chances."

"We understand," Carole said. "Don't worry, you can count on us."

Garvey didn't look terribly reassured, but he shrugged again and pointed with one huge finger to the stall behind Stevie. "That's Cookie Cutter right over there. She's our star, or at least she will be if she performs tomorrow like everyone thinks she will—knock on wood." As he spoke, the trainer reached out and rapped on the wooden wall with his massive fist.

Lisa turned with her friends to look where the trainer had pointed. Cookie Cutter was peering back at them out of her stall. She was a chestnut filly with a gleaming reddish gold coat and a wide white blaze down her intelligent face. The stall was open except for a barrier of webbing, so the girls could see almost every inch of the gorgeous Thoroughbred, from the tips of her alert ears to her delicate ankles and hooves. "Oh, she's beautiful!" Lisa exclaimed. She took a step forward, then hesitated. Some racehorses could be high-strung or even nasty. Just because Cookie Cutter looked sweet and friendly didn't necessarily mean she was. "Um, is it safe to pet her?"

"Sure," Garvey said with another of his massive shrugs. "She's friendly enough. But if you really want to win her over, feed her a few of these." He reached into a bucket hanging nearby and pulled out several large, crisp, pale-green leaves.

"What is it?" Carole asked, gingerly taking one of the leaves.

Garvey grinned, revealing several big gaps where teeth used to be. "Cabbage," he replied. "She loves the stuff."

He was right. The filly eagerly gobbled down every one of the cabbage leaves The Saddle Club offered her. Then she nuzzled the girls, looking for more.

16

Lisa laughed. "Whoa, girl," she said, gently extricating the edge of her T-shirt from the filly's mouth. "Save room for lunch!"

By this time Garvey had wandered off to talk to the jockey again. The two men were standing near the far end of the row of stalls. "What do you think of your subject, Deborah?" Stevie asked, glancing down the aisle to make sure the huge man wasn't close enough to hear her. "I bet you never expected to interview The Incredible Hulk."

"Stevie!" Deborah chided. Then she giggled. "I guess I should have mentioned that Garvey was a heavyweight boxer before he started training horses."

"That explains the missing teeth," Carole said. "I just assumed he got kicked in the face by a horse or something."

Stevie reached up to stroke Cookie Cutter's soft nose. "Maybe he did," she said. "I think the polite part of his personality got kicked out of him along with his teeth."

Deborah shook her head. "Come on, Stevie. He's not that bad. Put yourself in his shoes. This is the first time he's had sole responsibility for part of the Maskee string. It's a big job, and he's probably nervous—especially since this girl is getting ready for her debut." She reached up to give Cookie Cutter a friendly slap on the neck. Then she looked at her watch. "I'd better get going," she said. "I've got to pick up some information in the track steward's office. Will you be okay by yourselves?"

"No problem," Stevie assured her. "We'll be right at home."

17

After Deborah hurried off, the girls spent a few more minutes with Cookie Cutter, who seemed happy with the attention.

Finally Lisa said, "I guess we should go find one of the grooms and offer to make ourselves useful." The bay colt was back in his stall and the groom was nowhere in sight. Garvey and the jockey had also disappeared.

"Uh-huh." It was clear that Carole hadn't even heard her. She was too busy looking the horse over from stem to stern. "Can you believe her conformation? Look at how straight her hind legs are."

Stevie gave her a funny look. "Were you expecting them to be crooked?"

"No, look at them from the side. See? A straight hind leg is a big plus in a racehorse," Carole said. She had read that in a book she had taken out of the library recently, and she continued to explain as the girls headed away from the stall in search of the groom. "It helps her run faster. That straight hind leg means she can propel herself forward more powerfully and efficiently."

"Really?" Lisa said. She paused to peer into the makeshift tack room that had been set up in one of the stalls. Nobody was there.

"She's right," said a voice from behind the girls. "Hi, I'm Josh Winfield. Who are you?"

The Saddle Club turned and saw a boy about their age standing in the aisle. He was dressed in boots and jeans almost as worn out as Stevie's and a faded Kentucky Derby T-shirt.

The girls introduced themselves. "We're just visiting," Lisa said.

"For visitors, you seem to know a lot about racing," Josh said, giving Carole an admiring look.

Stevie grinned. "Well, some of us, anyway," she said. "Carole's our resident expert on anything and everything horse-related."

"But I don't actually know much about racing," Carole put in quickly. She didn't want the friendly boy to think she was bragging. "Do you work here?"

"Assistant groom at Bartlett Stables right here in Kentucky," Josh replied proudly. He smiled at Carole, revealing a mouthful of braces. "When I'm not in school, that is. I help out at the farm before and after school during the year, and in the summer I get to go to the track with the racers."

"That is so cool!" Stevie exclaimed.

Carole thought so, too, but she didn't say anything. Something about the way Josh was looking at her made her feel a little shy.

"You must know a lot about racing," Lisa said to Josh.

He nodded. "I guess I do," he said. "My dad trains the yearlings at Bartlett, so I've been around the sport all my life. I want to be a jockey when I get older, if I don't get too big. Otherwise I'll probably be a trainer, like my dad." He glanced at Carole again and took a step closer. "How did you learn so much about horses, Carole?"

Carole shrugged and took a step away. She liked Josh, but he was definitely making her nervous, and she still wasn't sure why. "I've been riding since I was little."

"What kind of riding do you do?" Josh took a larger step toward her, smiling eagerly. "English? Western?"

"English, mostly." Carole held her ground this time, deciding that she was being silly. Josh was just being friendly. "I really don't know much about racing at all."

"But we can't wait to see some action tomorrow," Stevie said. "Especially Cookie Cutter's race."

"Cookie Cutter?" Josh said. "Oh, you mean that chestnut filly down the aisle. She's getting a whole lot of talk for an untested two-year-old." He grinned. "My boss isn't scared, though. We've got a filly who's going to beat the bridle off her tomorrow."

"Oh, really?" Josh's words sounded like a challenge, and there was nothing Stevie liked more than a challenge. "Who says?"

"I says," Josh returned with a good-natured laugh. "Our filly's called Leprechaun. She's got amazing early speed and a heart of gold."

"Leprechaun is in the same race as Cookie Cutter?" Lisa asked.

"That's right," Josh said. But Lisa noticed he was looking at Carole as he said it. "It's a maiden race. That means only horses that have never won a race can enter. But I'm sure tomorrow will be the last time Leprechaun will be eligible for one of those."

Carole already knew what a maiden race was, but she didn't say anything. She could tell Josh was trying to show off for the visitors. Or was he just trying to show off for her? He had hardly taken his eyes off her since he joined them, and she couldn't help noticing that most of his comments seemed to be directed at her rather than her friends.

"Are you Leprechaun's groom?" Stevie asked.

"Not exactly," Josh admitted, looking away from Carole long enough to answer Stevie's question. "But I help her regular groom a lot. He's even going to let me walk along with him when he leads her to the paddock tomorrow before the race." He smiled proudly. "If she wins, maybe I'll get to go to the winner's circle, too." He turned and gave Carole a conspiratorial wink. "But my most important job is to remind the jockey not to use his whip on her during the race. We're afraid he'll slip up and automatically go for it in the stretch, and that would be a disaster."

It was a strange comment, and it made Carole so curious that she forgot about her nervousness for a moment. "Really?" she asked. "Why can't he use the whip on her?" She and her friends knew that a jockey's whip, used properly, didn't hurt the horse. It was just a way to direct the horse during a race, to get it to run faster or pay attention to its rider.

"She hates it." Josh shrugged. "Nobody knows why. Maybe she has extra-sensitive skin or something. Every time someone touches her with the whip, or even holds it where she can see it, she either stops dead in her tracks or bolts across the track. Luckily we found that out before she started racing."

The three girls nodded solemnly. They knew that a horse that reacted either of those ways during a race could cause a serious accident.

"It's a heck of a personality quirk, all right," Josh said. He grinned at Carole again. "I don't know about the horses you ride, but it sometimes seems like racehorses make an effort to come up with weirder and weirder habits to drive us humans crazy. For instance, there's another filly in the race tomorrow that won't go to sleep until her groom kisses her goodnight. One of the colts from your stable is famous for trying to throw the first exercise boy who gets on him each day. He'll let anybody ride him the rest of the time, but if you're the first one aboard in the morning, look out! One of our colts back at Bartlett refuses to walk onto the track with a lead pony. Most horses like having another horse there to keep them calm just before a race, but he just hates sharing the spotlight. Half our ponies have big bite marks on their necks, thanks to him."

Lisa shook her head. It still amazed her sometimes to discover that horses had such distinctive personalities. "Wow," she said. "That makes Cookie Cutter's cabbage habit seem almost normal."

"Speaking of Cookie Cutter," Stevie said, glancing down the row, "isn't that her heading out right now?"

The others looked just in time to see Garvey leading the chestnut filly out of the shed with a light racing saddle on her back. "I guess it's her turn to work," Carole said.

"That's right," Josh said, giving her a big smile. "See? I could tell right away you knew your way around the track."

Lisa and Stevie kept quiet. Carole's comment hadn't been especially brilliant—anyone could guess Cookie Cutter was going out to the track for some exercise—but Josh certainly seemed to be impressed.

"Come on," Stevie said. "Let's go watch. Our chores can wait another few minutes."

"Mine can't," Josh said reluctantly. "I've been gone too long already. But I hope I'll see you around." He smiled at Carole, then seemed to remember the other two girls. "Um, all of you, I mean. Bye."

Stevie and Lisa contained themselves until Josh had disappeared. Then they burst out laughing.

"Carole and Josh, sittin' in a tree . . . ," Stevie sang.

Carole blushed. "Stop it," she said. "I don't know what you're talking about."

"Then why are you blushing?" Lisa asked with a grin. "Come on, Carole. It's obvious the guy is gaga over you."

Carole shook her head. She wasn't disagreeing with what Lisa was saying, but she didn't really understand it. "It's a little weird, don't you think? I mean, he doesn't even know me."

"I don't think it's weird at all," Stevie said loyally. "Any boy in his right mind would naturally fall in love with you at first sight. I'm surprised it doesn't happen all the time."

Carole shook her head again. "I just don't get it," she said. She didn't have as much experience with boys as either of her friends, and sometimes the things they did confused her.

She decided to forget about Josh's bizarre behavior. There were much more interesting things to think about at the racetrack. "Come on, let's go catch up to Cookie Cutter or we'll miss seeing her run."

3

THE GIRLS REACHED the track just in time to see Cookie Cutter start cantering. All around the wide oval dirt surface, other horses and riders were walking, cantering, or running, either alone or in groups of two or three. But the girls were able to spot the Maskee filly's bright chestnut coat and white face almost immediately. The small man Garvey had been talking to earlier was perched high on her back.

Stevie soon spotted Garvey himself leaning against the rail nearby. Deborah was next to him, looking very small by comparison. "I guess Deborah finished her errand," Stevie commented. "Come on, let's go watch with them."

The Saddle Club joined the two adults at the rail and looked back toward Cookie Cutter just in time to see her break into a run. "Wow!" Carole exclaimed. "Look at her go!"

Even running by herself, the filly was impressive. Her long, slender legs flashed forward rhythmically and her nostrils flared slightly as her head stretched out in front of her. She looked thrilled to be running and eager to show everyone how fast she was.

It was over all too soon. After he had taken her just a short distance around the track, the jockey pulled her up. Cookie Cutter shook her head a little, obviously disappointed. But after a moment she obediently slowed to a canter, then to a walk. Her rider turned her and rode slowly back in the direction of the spectators at the rail.

"That was great," Lisa said. "Even though it was kind of short. How long is the race she's in tomorrow?"

Garvey just stared at the horse coming toward him. He seemed to be pretending not to have heard Lisa's question, even though there was no way he could have missed it.

Deborah cleared her throat. "I was wondering the same thing, Garvey," she said loudly. "How long is tomorrow's race?"

"Six furlongs," Garvey replied shortly.

The Saddle Club exchanged glances. They had heard the term *furlong* before while at the track, and they knew that it was a way of measuring distance, but even Carole wasn't exactly sure what it meant. Somehow none of them felt like asking Garvey to explain.

"Do you think she's well prepped for the race?" Deborah asked Garvey, her pen poised over the small notepad she was holding.

26

"If she wasn't prepared, she wouldn't be running," Garvey replied with a frown.

Deborah didn't seem taken aback by the rude answer. The Saddle Club guessed that she was used to interviewing difficult subjects. "Of course," she said smoothly. "Can you tell me a little about her training, then?"

Garvey sighed heavily. "Not unless you have all day. Training a racehorse is a complicated business, in case you didn't realize it."

"I'm sure it is," Deborah said. She smiled. "Even more complicated than boxing, right?"

Garvey frowned and gave Deborah a sharp look. "If you're here to ask me about my past, you can forget it," he said brusquely. "Your boss said you were coming to talk about horse racing, and that's all I'm interested in talking about."

"All right, then, we'll stick to horse racing," Deborah said. By now she was starting to look a tiny bit annoyed, though someone who didn't know her well might not have noticed it. The Saddle Club noticed, though, and they didn't blame her one bit. "It would be helpful to have a little background information on you for the story. But we'll stay away from boxing if you prefer." She glanced down at her notepad. "So how about an easy one: Where are you from originally, Garvey?"

This time the large man didn't hesitate. In fact, he looked almost relieved at the question. "I was born and raised in Dry River, Virginia."

27

"I guess that *was* an easy one," Stevie said under her breath, and Carole and Lisa tried not to laugh.

Just then Cookie Cutter pulled up in front of them. "Did she feel all right, Toby?" Garvey called to the rider, turning his back on Deborah before she could ask any more questions.

"Sure thing," the little man replied. Stevie noticed he had a slightly worried expression on his face. "Are you sure about the distance, though? I could take her another couple of furlongs. The boss seemed to think—"

Garvey cut him off angrily. "*I'm* the boss while we're here, okay?" he growled. "You're just the jockey. That means you follow my orders. And don't you forget it."

Toby gave in immediately. "Okay, okay," he said. "Sorry—I wasn't trying to second-guess you." He reached down and gave the filly's neck a pat. "I just want good old C.C. here to win tomorrow, that's all."

"We all do," Garvey said, sounding calmer. "And she will if our luck holds." He smiled slightly. "If I were a betting man, I'd have money on her tomorrow. And that's a genuine tip." Noticing that the girls were hanging on his every word, he added, "For anyone here who's old enough to gamble, that is."

"Don't you bet on your horses?" Carole asked. She knew Mr. McLeod and others from Maskee Farms often bet money on their own horses if they thought they would win.

Garvey shook his head. "I don't bet on anyone's horses," he said. "I may be the only one around this place who

28

doesn't, but that's the way I was raised." He shrugged. "Besides, just keeping these critters healthy and trying to get them ready to run is enough of a gamble for me."

Deborah made a note on her pad. Meanwhile, Lisa was looking toward the break in the rail where the horses entered the track. "Hey, look," she said. "Isn't that Josh?"

Carole looked up just as Josh spotted her. He was too far away to call to her, but he waved wildly, grinning from ear to ear. He was so enthusiastic that several other people turned to see who had his attention. Even the horse he was leading, a tall gray filly, swiveled her head around to look in the girls' direction. Stevie and Lisa waved back, and Carole lifted her hand shyly.

"I wonder if that's the horse he was talking about before," Stevie said. "What was her name?"

"Leprechaun," Carole supplied. "She's running against Cookie Cutter tomorrow."

Toby heard her and looked over at the gray. "That's Leprechaun, all right," he confirmed. Stevie was pleased to notice that, unlike Garvey, the jockey talked to them like people, not like little kids. "She looks to be the only real competition for C.C. tomorrow. I've been watching her work, and if anyone gives us a run for the money, she'll be the one. Especially if the racing luck is on her side instead of ours."

Garvey frowned at the comment. "Don't just let that horse stand there in her own sweat," he said sharply. "She's got to be cooled down. Toby, show these girls what to do, and don't be long about it. I need you to breeze the bay colt sometime this century."

"Sure thing, boss," Toby said, his face expressionless. He turned and rode Cookie Cutter toward the gap in the fence, gesturing for the girls to meet him there.

The Saddle Club said good-bye to Deborah and walked to meet the horse and jockey. "Boy, Deborah really has her work cut out for her, doesn't she?" Lisa commented quietly. "Garvey doesn't seem too thrilled about being interviewed."

Stevie nodded. "Just about the only question he answered without scowling was the one about where he was from. And that was an easy one, like Deborah said."

"Not necessarily," Carole put in with a smile. "For me, that question would be almost as complicated as the one about Cookie Cutter's training."

Her friends laughed. Carole's father was a colonel in the Marine Corps, and her family had moved around from base to base before settling for good in Willow Creek.

Toby and Cookie Cutter were waiting for them by the gap. "Sorry about Garvey's temper," the jockey said. He had dismounted, and once they were standing beside him the girls could see that he wasn't much taller than they were. "He's always kind of tense, and he's been worse than ever since he got to Bluegrass. And if your friend mentioned his boxing career it probably didn't help. He's kind of sensitive about that topic." He smiled. "He also seems to have forgotten whatever manners his mama might have taught him. Who *are* you three, anyway? I know the woman with you is a newspaper reporter, but . . ."

The Saddle Club laughed. Then, as all of them walked back toward the shed row with Cookie Cutter in tow, Carole quickly introduced the three of them and explained why they were there.

"I see," Toby said, stroking his chin thoughtfully. "Your riding instructor wanted to get you out of his hair, so he sent you out here to get in ours."

Stevie shot him a quick glance, but one look at his face assured her that he was kidding. "That's right," she retorted. "And we're going to prove it by asking you a million questions about racing."

"I'm game," Toby said. "Ask away."

"Okay," Stevie said. "Why's Garvey so sensitive about his boxing career?"

Toby raised one eyebrow and glanced at her. "I don't know him real well, but I hear he wasn't too successful as a boxer, so he doesn't like to be reminded of that part of his life." He smiled. "Is that what you call a racing question?"

"I've got one. A real racing question, I mean," Lisa spoke up. "What on earth is a furlong?"

Toby looked surprised for a second, then burst out laughing. "I guess that's a fair question," he said, pausing for a moment to let Cookie Cutter sniff at some low-hanging tree

31

branches near the path. "We all get so used to hearing that term around here that it's easy to forget people don't use it all the time."

"It's a unit of measurement, right?" Carole asked.

Toby nodded. "Exactly right," he said. "One furlong is equal to one-eighth of a mile, or two hundred and twenty yards." He waved a hand behind him to indicate the track. "For instance, Bluegrass Park's racetrack is a mile and a quarter around. But it would be the same thing to say it's ten furlongs."

"So a six-furlong race is really . . . um . . . three-quarters of a mile," Lisa said, calculating quickly in her head.

"That's right," Toby replied. "That's how far C.C. is running tomorrow."

"C.C. is a cute nickname," Stevie said. "Have you been riding her long?"

"Not that long," Toby said. By this time they had reached the rows of stables and were walking toward their own. They paused again to allow the curious filly to watch a stable cat wander by. "She hasn't raced yet, as you probably know. Garvey had an exercise boy riding her in the mornings until this week. But he wanted me to get used to her before race day, so here I am."

Carole noticed that he was frowning just a little as he spoke, and she suspected she knew why. She didn't want to seem nosy, but the jockey seemed so down-to-earth that she couldn't resist asking. "What was all that stuff about the distance of the workout? You didn't seem very happy about it."

Toby smiled ruefully. "Perceptive, aren't you?" he said. "But you're right. I was worried because the boss—the head trainer, that is—had laid out a rough training schedule for C.C. leading up to the race, and Garvey has been doing his own thing all week. He's changed some of the distances of the workouts and adjusted the schedule in other ways."

"Is that bad?" Lisa asked.

"Well, there's more than one way to get a horse ready to run. But the boss usually knows what he's doing." Toby shrugged and sighed. "Maybe Garvey does, too. I hope so."

They walked into the barn with the filly in tow, and the girls quickly helped Toby remove her tack. "Shouldn't you be hurrying back to the track?" Carole asked, feeling a little worried on the jockey's behalf. "Garvey seemed awfully eager for you to exercise that other horse." *And*, she added silently to herself, *Garvey seems like a bad person to make angry*.

Toby laughed. "That's just Garvey being Garvey," he said. "Naturally you wouldn't recognize them, but there were two other Maskee horses on the track waiting their turn for Garvey's attention when we left. I'll be back with the bay colt in plenty of time."

"You mean you don't ride all of Maskee's horses?" Stevie

asked, watching as the jockey pulled out a light blanket and snapped it onto the chestnut filly's back.

Toby shook his head. "Unless we're preparing for an important race, I usually don't ride for Maskee in the mornings at all," he said. "Garvey hires exercise boys to do that." He gave the girls a wink and handed Cookie Cutter's lead line to Carole. "I grab any chance I can get to sleep in."

He said good-bye and strolled down the aisle, where one of the grooms was waiting with the bay colt the girls had seen earlier. Now the horse was tacked up and ready to go, and Toby led him away in the direction of the track.

The girls started walking in a big circle around the shed row. Carole led Cookie Cutter, and Stevie and Lisa walked alongside to keep her company.

"There's so much interesting stuff going on here, isn't there?" Carole mused.

Stevie nodded. "Especially when it comes to Garvey," she said. "I think there might be something mysterious about him."

"Huh?" Lisa and Carole said in one voice, looking at their friend in surprise.

"Think about it," Stevie said. "He doesn't want to answer any of Deborah's questions, especially questions about his past. He's mean and surly to just about everyone. He's been changing his boss's training schedule. What does all that tell you?"

"It tells me you've been watching too many TV detective shows," Carole said with a laugh. "Although no self-

34

respecting TV detective would get involved in anything with those pathetic clues."

Lisa grinned. "Actually, maybe Stevie's having a flashback to our last trip to the racetrack," she told Carole. "She remembers that we solved a mystery then, and she thinks we'll probably stumble over another one here."

"Maybe." Carole tried to keep a straight face. "But what are the odds of that?"

Stevie's face was bright red by now. "Okay, enough. You two are pretty funny. But I have a hunch about this. Something's weird about Garvey."

Lisa shrugged. "Nobody's arguing with you there," she said. "But there's nothing particularly mysterious about being weird and antisocial."

Just then they noticed a wiry young man walking toward them leading two sweaty horses. "Are you the Maskee hotwalkers?" he called out.

"I guess those are our next customers," Lisa said. "Come on, Stevie. Let's go untack them."

As her friends hurried off, Carole continued to walk with Cookie Cutter. She was just rounding the far corner of the shed row when she heard someone calling her name. She turned and saw Josh coming toward her, a big smile on his face.

"Hi there," he said. "I see you get to walk the star." He jerked his thumb at Cookie Cutter. "Does that mean you're the star hot-walker?"

Carole wasn't sure how to answer that. She suspected it

35

was the kind of question that didn't require an answer, so she just shrugged. "Where's Leprechaun?" she asked. "I saw her going onto the track. Don't you have to walk her after her workout?"

"Nope," Josh replied, falling into step beside her as she continued around the path. "We have hot-walkers, too, you know. I just took her back to the barn and untacked her. She'll be walking for at least half an hour, so I figured I'd come over here and see what you were doing."

"Well, now you see it," Carole said with a weak smile.

Josh laughed as if it were the funniest thing anyone had ever said. "You're really clever, Carole," he said, looking at her admiringly. "By the way, that's a really pretty name."

For a second Carole thought he was talking about Cookie Cutter's name. Then she realized he meant *her* name, and she blushed. Why had this boy suddenly decided to start mooning over her? She definitely didn't get it, and she wasn't sure she liked it.

Josh reached out to pat Cookie Cutter on the neck. "She looked good out there this morning," he said. "She's a nice filly. I'm almost sorry we're going to beat her tomorrow."

"Don't be so sure about that," Carole returned with a smile, feeling slightly relieved at the change in topic. She felt on firmer ground talking about horses than she did talking about herself. "Cookie Cutter told me herself that she's planning to win that race."

"Oh yeah?" Josh said with a laugh. "Well, I would never contradict such a lovely pair of ladies. So I guess we'll just have to wait and see what happens. Sometimes it all comes down to racing luck."

Carole blushed some more at the compliment. This was definitely weird. Still, she had a job to do, and nothing was going to stop her from doing it—not even a moony-eyed boy.

Realizing that Josh had used the same term Toby had used earlier, she looked at the boy curiously. "You racetrack people seem to talk about racing luck a lot."

"I suppose we do," Josh said, looking rather surprised at the thought. "But it's only because it's such an important factor. No matter what we do to get these beasts ready, just about anything can happen once we set them loose in a race. So it helps to have luck on your side." He shrugged. "That's why we have so many superstitions around here." He tugged at his T-shirt and smiled a little sheepishly. "For instance, I always wear this on any day one of our horses is running. That means I'll be wearing it again tomorrow, as you may notice if we see each other." His sheepish grin faded into an adoring smile. "And I sure hope we do. See each other, I mean."

Carole smiled back a little uncertainly. She couldn't help feeling a tiny bit flattered by Josh's attention. Stevie had a boyfriend named Phil, and Lisa occasionally went on dates with boys from school. Carole had dated, but she had always been a lot more interested in horses and riding than boys. She wasn't expecting that to change anytime soon, but maybe she should look on the positive side. Maybe this weekend at the track would be a chance to find out what all the fuss was about.

4

THERE WAS A lull in the racetrack bustle at around ten-thirty. The Saddle Club had walked all of the Maskee horses after their workouts, then pitched in to help with the other stable chores. Finally everything was finished—for the moment.

"You three might as well grab some lunch," Garvey told them. "By the way," he added gruffly, "you're pretty good workers—for a bunch of girls, anyway." He hurried away before The Saddle Club could answer.

Carole looked surprised. "I'm not sure, but I think that might have been a compliment."

"I think you're right," Lisa said. "And I think we deserved it. I also think Garvey was right about lunch. It may be early, but I'm starved."

Deborah found them in the cafeteria a little while later.

39

The girls had already gobbled down huge lunches and were now busy sipping at the remains of their sodas and talking about everything that had happened that morning.

"There you are," Deborah said. "I had a feeling I might find you here. How would you like to see something interesting?"

The girls were all ears. "What is it?" Carole asked.

"Cookie Cutter is about to be okayed out of the gate," Deborah said. Seeing the girls' confused expressions, she laughed. "Since she's never raced before, the track starter has to watch her break from the starting gate so he knows she can do it properly during a race. Want to come see?"

"Of course we do," Stevie said, jumping to her feet.

The girls followed Deborah back toward the track. "I can't believe Garvey never told us this was happening," Carole said. "He just sent us off for lunch and never mentioned it."

Deborah glanced at her over her shoulder. "I'm not surprised, for two reasons," she said. "For one thing, Cookie Cutter really should have been okayed before this—especially since she's already been worked today. Most trainers wouldn't time things like this, since the horse could be so tired out by all the exercise that she's not in top shape for her race. Garvey is really leaving things to the last minute, and I get the distinct feeling it's because he plain forgot to do it earlier in the week."

"Yikes," Carole said. "What's the second reason?"

Deborah smiled. "It probably never occurred to him that

40

you'd be interested," she said. "In case you haven't noticed, he's not a very gracious host."

Stevie rolled her eyes. "Believe me, we've noticed."

When the group reached the grandstand rail, they saw that the starting gate was just being set up on the track nearby. It was a large metal structure, with about a dozen separate starting stalls. A huge tractor pulled it into place. During longer races, the girls knew, the tractor was also used to take the gate out of the way before the horses rounded the track.

"Look, there's C.C.," Carole said, pointing. The filly was prancing just inside the gap. Toby was on her back, patting her and talking to her soothingly.

"I see you're on a nickname basis with her already," Deborah said with a laugh. "Why doesn't that surprise me?"

They all leaned on the rail and watched as Toby rode the chestnut filly toward the back of the starting gate. The back doors of all the stalls were standing open and ready, and Toby aimed C.C. toward one near the middle. Two other men were standing nearby, watching carefully.

"Those are the assistant starters," Deborah told the girls. "They're there to help load the horse into the gate if necessary."

But it wasn't necessary to help Cookie Cutter. She paused for a second just outside the narrow stall, but at a little urging from Toby, she carefully stepped forward, then stood quietly inside as one of the assistant starters closed the door behind her.

There was a second's pause; then a bell rang and the front doors of the starting gate clanged open. Cookie Cutter sprang forward and raced a short way down the track before Toby pulled her up, patting her on the withers and looking pleased.

"She did that like a real pro," Carole said admiringly.

Deborah nodded, but she looked distracted. "She sure did," she said. "Look, there's Garvey. I'm going to try to catch up to him now while he's not too busy. I'll meet you back at the shed row, okay?"

Deborah had hardly hurried away when someone else took her place. It was a tall, thin boy who looked a few years older than the Saddle Club girls. He was wearing khaki pants and a clean white shirt.

"Hello," he said. "I hope you don't mind me coming over like this, but I couldn't help noticing you here. Please allow me to introduce myself. My name is Josh. Josh Parker."

"Really?" Stevie blurted out in surprise before she could stop herself.

The boy looked a little confused, but he nodded. "I'm working here at the track for the summer. I hadn't seen you girls around before, so I thought I'd come over and say hello."

Stevie and Lisa exchanged glances. Josh's words seemed to be directed at all of them, but he was looking at only one of them—Carole.

"We've never been here before," Stevie told him. "We're

just visiting for the weekend. I'm Stevie, and this is my friend Lisa. And this is our friend, Carole. Carole Hanson."

"Carole," Josh said with a smile. "What a pretty name."

Lisa giggled, and Stevie kicked her. "Oh yes," Stevie told Josh with a straight face. "It's a beautiful name. We're all just green with envy about it."

Josh didn't seem to hear her, but Carole did. She shot Stevie a very dirty look. "Um, what do you do here at the track, Josh?" she asked. "Are you a groom or something?" Judging by the cleanliness of his clothes, she doubted it.

"Nope," Josh replied. "I can hardly tell one end of a horse from the other, I'm afraid. I mostly help out selling tickets at the front gate, but sometimes I fill in at the snack bar or the program booth. My uncle is the track manager here. He got me a part-time job as soon as I turned sixteen this past spring."

"Sixteen, hmm?" Stevie murmured. "An older man . . ." This time she spoke quietly enough so that neither Carole nor Josh caught her words. But Lisa heard them. She giggled again, and Carole definitely heard that. Her blush grew deeper.

"Where are you all from?" Josh asked. Once again, he looked only at Carole as he said it.

"We're from Willow Creek, Virginia," Lisa supplied helpfully, noticing that Carole looked rather tongue-tied. "We all ride together at a stable there."

"That's terrific," Josh said, still staring at Carole. He

hardly seemed to notice that she wasn't the one who had spoken. "I bet you're really good riders. That's just terrific."

"Look, it's really nice to meet you, um, Josh," Carole said quickly. "But we have to go. We're helping out a friend with his horses, and I'm sure he needs us to walk the one that just broke out of the starting gate."

Lisa gave Stevie an amused glance. Carole must be desperate to get away from her new admirer if she was calling Garvey a friend.

"Okay," Josh said reluctantly. "Maybe I'll see you around later. You did say you were here for the whole weekend, right?"

"Right," Stevie confirmed. "See you around." The girls hurried away. As soon as they were out of earshot, Stevie turned to Carole with a grin. "What do you think of that?" she said.

Lisa laughed. "*Two* Joshes in one day, and they both like Carole. What are the odds of that?"

Carole sighed. "I don't know," she said. "But I think it's pretty weird. I don't look any better or worse than either of you. Why would a guy pick one of us over the others when he doesn't know *any* of us?"

"Love works in mysterious ways," Stevie replied.

Carole rolled her eyes. "Come on," she said, purposely changing the subject. She would have to think more about these strange developments later. "Let's go walk C.C." Even though the filly hadn't run very far after her break from the gate, Carole knew that she would need to be cooled down and groomed as carefully as if she'd just raced in the Kentucky Derby.

When they reached the shed row, the filly was already unsaddled and blanketed. Toby was walking her around the row, with Deborah beside him.

"We'll take over if you want," Lisa offered, hurrying up to take the horse's lead line.

"Thanks," Toby said, handing it to her. But he and Deborah continued to walk with the girls. "Deborah told me you saw C.C.'s debut out of the gate."

Carole nodded. "It was very interesting. I never really thought about it before, but it must take some careful training to get them to do that."

"Sure it does," the jockey replied. "Anything you want a horse to do requires training—except maybe eating."

The girls laughed. They all knew how true that was. "Well, C.C. seems to have learned her lessons pretty well," Lisa said, giving the filly a pat on the nose.

"She's a good horse," Toby said. "With luck, she'll prove that to everyone tomorrow by winning the race." Smiling, he reached up and rapped on his skull with one fist. "Knock on wood."

"I hope she does well," Deborah said. "I was talking to Leprechaun's trainer—he's another one of my story subjects—and he's pretty confident about his own horse."

Toby chuckled. "Sure he is, and he should be. That's what horse racing is all about. I'm sure Garvey is just as confident about C.C."

"I wouldn't know," Deborah muttered.

Lisa noticed her anxious expression. "Isn't Garvey answering your questions?"

Deborah shrugged. "Some of them," she said. "The trouble is, I'd planned to make him the centerpiece of my story. I figured that since he was from Maskee Farms, I'd be able to follow up with him back home—you know, add some human interest stuff . . ."

Stevie nodded wisely. "Too bad. You found out he's not human."

That made Deborah laugh. "He's not *that* bad," she admitted. "Still, I wish he would be a little more forthcoming."

"Well, if there's anything I can tell you to fill in the gaps, just let me know," Toby said. "I've ridden Mr. McLeod's horses for a long time, so I'm pretty familiar with his whole operation, even the mysterious Garvey Cannon."

Stevie suddenly looked interested. "It's funny you should use that word, *mysterious* . . . ," she began.

But Toby didn't hear her. He had just spotted a slender young woman hurrying along nearby. "Hey, there's the trainer I was telling you about," he told Deborah. "I really think you should talk to her for your article. Do you want me to introduce you?"

"Definitely," Deborah said. "With Garvey not talking, I've got plenty of space to fill. See you later, girls."

The two adults hurried off to catch up to the trainer,

leaving the girls with Cookie Cutter. "Now," Stevie said, turning to grin at Carole, "I think it's time for a Saddle Club meeting. We have to talk about this very interesting situation with Carole and her not-so-secret admirers."

Before the others could reply, Josh—the first one— rounded the corner of the shed row and spotted them. He hurried toward them, smiling gleefully.

"Uh-oh, here comes one of them now," Stevie muttered. "We're going to have to start calling them Josh A and Josh B."

Lisa giggled just as Josh A reached them. "What's so funny?" he asked.

"Oh, nothing," Lisa said quickly. "Um, Stevie was just telling us a joke."

"Really? Let's hear it," Josh said. "I love a good joke."

Stevie thought fast. "What has four legs and eats off the floor?"

"What?" Josh asked.

"A horse with no stable manners," Stevie replied. "Get it? Stable manners . . ."

Josh laughed. "That's pretty funny," he said. He turned to look at Carole. "Do you know any jokes, Carole?"

"No," Carole said, carefully keeping her eyes trained on Cookie Cutter rather than meeting Josh's adoring gaze. "I don't like jokes."

At that, Lisa rolled her eyes and Stevie snorted. Carole liked a good joke as much as anyone, if not more.

"You're more the serious type, huh?" Josh said, nodding agreeably. "I admire that. I could tell you were kind of quiet and thoughtful from the moment I first saw you."

Stevie and Lisa could hardly keep straight faces at that. Carole might be considered thoughtful, at least if you defined *thoughtful* as thinking about horses day and night. But quiet? Never.

Before Carole could come up with an answer, she heard another voice calling her name.

"There you are," Josh B said, running up to them. Cookie Cutter snorted a little at his approach and took a step backward.

"Careful," Carole said quickly. "It's not a good idea to run around horses. Some of them spook easily."

"Sorry," Josh B said, looking chagrined. He gave Carole an apologetic smile. "My uncle has told me that a million times. I guess I was so excited to see you that I forgot."

"I don't think we've met," Josh A said, stepping forward. His normally cheerful look had been replaced with a suspicious one. He stuck out his hand. "Josh Winfield, Bartlett Stables."

Josh B shook his hand, looking just as suspicious as he glanced from Josh A to Carole and back again. "Josh Parker, Bluegrass Park."

"Uh-oh," Stevie whispered to Lisa. "Showdown at the Josh Corral."

Cookie Cutter had calmed down as soon as Josh B had

48

stopped running, and Lisa quickly had her moving again. The whole group trailed along beside her.

"So, you work here?" Josh A asked Josh B.

Josh B nodded. "I was just telling Carole about it a little while ago," he said, turning to smile at Carole. "Right, Carole?"

"Um, right," Carole said.

"I was telling her about my job, too," Josh A said quickly. "I'm working with some of the top horses at this meet. Maybe you've heard of some of them. Leprechaun, Speedy Bee—"

Josh B cut him off with a shrug. "I don't really have the time to keep up with every single horse that runs here," he said. "I'm too busy making sure the whole track runs smoothly."

Lisa raised an eyebrow. Manning the snack bar didn't seem all that critical to her. On the other hand, she noticed that Josh A hadn't bothered to mention that he was only a part-time assistant groom. Instead, he seemed to want Josh B to think he was training the entire Bartlett Stables string himself.

Lisa glanced at Carole and saw that she looked as uncomfortable as Lisa had ever seen her. It was time to do something about the situation. As amusing as it might be to her and to Stevie, Carole obviously wasn't having any fun.

"Hey, Carole," Lisa said. "Isn't it about time for you to go inside and take care of that errand Garvey wanted you to do?"

"What?" Carole said. "Oh! I mean, yes, I think you're right. I'd better get going."

"What kind of errand?" Josh A asked.

"Perhaps I can help," Josh B added quickly.

"Um . . ." Carole looked at Lisa for help, but Lisa's mind was a blank.

Luckily, Stevie came to the rescue. "There's no time to stand around talking about it," she barked out, giving Carole a shove. "You're late already. Go, go, go!"

Carole didn't have to be told again. Even though she never ran when there were horses around, she broke into a brisk jog as soon as she was a safe distance from Cookie Cutter.

Lisa shot Stevie a grateful glance. Stevie grinned back. "So, boys," she said cheerfully. "Now that Carole's gone, I guess you'll just have to settle for talking to Lisa and me."

The Joshes looked at Stevie and Lisa. Then they both glanced in the direction Carole had gone. "Um, my uncle probably needs me in the office," Josh B mumbled, backing away.

Josh A nodded and looked at the ground. "I think I'd better get back to my barn," he added hastily. A second later, both boys were gone.

Lisa and Stevie continued to walk with Cookie Cutter, who seemed much more interested in the stray patches of grass along their route than in her human companions. "Call me crazy," Lisa said, "but Josh didn't seem to be heading toward his own barn."

Stevie nodded. "And the other Josh was going the opposite direction from the track office, unless they've suddenly moved it to an empty stall in the Maskee shed row."

"Where do you suppose they were going?" Lisa asked with a twinkle in her eye.

Stevie shrugged. "Beats me," she said. "But I think it's a good thing Carole had a head start!"

"THAT WAS GREAT, Deborah," Lisa said. "Thanks for letting us tag along."

"You're welcome," Deborah said, sinking deeper into the comfortable chair in the hotel lobby. It was early evening, and The Saddle Club and Deborah had just returned from an afternoon of touring some of Kentucky's horse country. Deborah had needed to visit several local racing and breeding stables for her research, and since the Maskee horses weren't in any races that afternoon, the girls had gone with her.

They had seen a lot of beautiful farms and even more gorgeous horses, from broodmares with their half-grown foals to retired stallions standing at stud. The owner of one stable had even invited them to watch some of his yearlings being trained. The frisky colts had already been taught to accept a bridle and saddle, and the yearling trainer was teaching them to accept a rider's weight. The Saddle Club had seen similar training sessions at Pine Hollow and elsewhere, but somehow it all seemed new and different here in Kentucky.

"I really liked that one yearling," Stevie mused. She was perched on a love seat next to Deborah's chair. Carole was next to her, and Lisa was standing nearby. They were waiting for a table at the hotel restaurant. A long day in the fresh summer air had made them all very hungry.

"Which one?" Carole asked.

Deborah grinned. "Let me guess," she said. "The bay with the white feet that kept trying to turn around and look at the guy who was riding him?"

"That's the one," Stevie confirmed. "He had a real sense of humor."

The others laughed. The clownish colt had been funny to watch, and it was no surprise that Stevie liked him.

"Most Thoroughbreds look so serious and businesslike on the racetrack," Carole said. "It's easy to forget that each one has its own unique personality."

"Speaking of unique personalities," Stevie said, lowering her voice, "check out the tourist convention across the way."

The others glanced at a group of seats nearby, where a family of three was clustered. The father was wearing shorts and a Hawaiian shirt. Two cameras hung around his neck, and he held a small, late-model camcorder in his hand. He was pointing it at his wife, who wore a Kentucky Horse Park T-shirt and floral shorts. She was posing for the camera with a boy about Lisa's age, who had to be her son. He was dressed in denim shorts and a T-shirt that matched his mother's.

Lisa and Deborah couldn't help giggling. "It looks like they're having a nice time in Kentucky," Carole said with a smile, giving the family one more glance.

As she did, the boy turned and met her eye. He looked surprised for a moment to catch her looking at him. Then he smiled.

"Uh-oh," Carole whispered, turning away quickly. "They caught me."

But it was too late. A moment later the boy was standing in front of her. He was holding one of his father's cameras.

"Hi there," he said. "I noticed you guys sitting here, and I was wondering if one of you would mind taking a picture so that my whole family can be in it together."

"Sure," Stevie said. "I'd be glad to."

She started to stand up, but the boy was already pushing the camera into Carole's hand. "This is totally cool of you. I—um, we—really appreciate it," he said, giving her a big smile.

"I don't know much about cameras," Carole protested. "Maybe Lisa should do it. She's the photographer here—"

"Don't worry. I'm sure you'll do an awesome job," the boy protested, extending a hand to help Carole to her feet. "By the way, my name's Josh. Josh Stanton."

54

"Hi, Josh," Carole said weakly. "I'm Carole." She followed him over to where his parents were waiting.

Stevie let out a low whistle. "This is really getting weird now," she told the others. The girls had filled Deborah in on Carole's two admirers during their drive that day.

Lisa nodded. "Could there really be *three* Joshes in Kentucky who all like Carole?"

"It sure looks that way," Deborah said. They turned to watch as Josh carefully posed his parents on one of the lobby sofas. Carole stood waiting, camera in hand, looking a little forlorn.

"I think we're going to have to come up with a new way to keep track of these guys," Stevie said after a moment, a twinkle in her eyes. "A, B, and C just doesn't have the Kentucky ring to it. Luckily, I have the perfect solution."

"Josh, Josher, and Joshest?" Lisa guessed.

"One potato, two potato, three potato?" Deborah asked.

"Nope. Even better." Stevie grinned. "Win, Place, and Show."

The others laughed. "Sounds good to me," Lisa said. "But which one is which? We don't know which of the Joshes Carole likes best."

"That's okay," Stevie said. "Josh A should be Win."

"Because his last name is Winfield?" Lisa asked.

Stevie shook her head. "Of course not," she said. "Because he came in first."

"So that must mean that the Josh grinning his head off over there right now is Show," Deborah guessed. "There's

55

just one problem with your brilliant idea, Stevie. What if a fourth Josh comes along?"

Stevie glanced over at Josh, who was sitting between his parents and smiling broadly at Carole as she tried to focus the complicated camera. "No way," she said firmly. "*Four* Joshes? Come on. What are the odds of *that*?"

They were still laughing when Carole rejoined them a moment later. "What's so funny?"

"We'll tell you when we get inside," Lisa said. She had just noticed the hostess gesturing to them. "It looks like our table is ready."

"I'll join you in a second," Deborah said as they all stood up. "I just remembered, I promised to call my editor when I got back. I'm just going to find a phone and then I'll be right in."

The girls ate rolls and talked about the Josh situation while they waited for Deborah. Stevie told Carole about her new names for the three boys, and Carole laughed. Then she turned serious again. "I just don't get it," she said once more.

"You don't have to understand it," Lisa advised her. "Just enjoy it. After this weekend, you'll never have to see any of them again if you don't want to."

"Thank goodness," Carole said, taking a sip of water. "I know I should be flattered, and I am, kind of. But I just don't know how to act when they're acting that way and I don't even know them. It's not at all like it was with Cam." Cam was a boy Carole had met through her computer. They had

56

chatted on-line about horses many times before they ever met, so Carole knew they had something in common. However, Cam's family had moved away before Carole could really start thinking of him as a boyfriend.

Just then Deborah returned. She was humming a little as she sat down. "Okay. That's taken care of," she said cheerfully.

Stevie gave her a suspicious look. "So, how's your editor doing?"

"Oh, she's just fine," Deborah replied with a big smile. "Very fine."

"Did Max get her down for her nap okay without you?" Stevie asked innocently.

"She fell asleep right away once he started singing to her—Oops." Deborah grinned sheepishly. "You caught me."

The Saddle Club laughed. "We understand," Lisa said. "We don't blame you for wanting to check in on Maxi."

"I really did call my editor first," Deborah said, reaching for a roll.

"Uh-huh," Stevie said. "We'll take your word for it. Right now, I'm much more interested in talking about food. And I don't mean baby food!"

The next forty minutes passed quickly as the group talked about everything they had done and seen that day. Before long, the topic turned to the next afternoon's races.

"I can't wait to watch C.C. break out of the starting gate in a real race," Stevie said.

Deborah nodded. "I just hope I'm back in time to see it.

I've got appointments at more farms tomorrow, and if all goes well, I'll barely get back to the track before post time. I really hope I make it."

Carole swallowed a big mouthful of mashed potatoes. "I hope you do, too," she said. "C.C. looked really great out there this morning. I'm sure she's going to . . . uh . . ." Her voice trailed off as she stared across the room.

"Win?" Stevie supplied helpfully.

"No," Carole said grimly. "Show." The others turned and saw the newest Josh and his parents taking their seats several tables away.

"Let's pretend we don't see them," Lisa suggested. "Maybe they won't notice you."

But they did. Before long, Carole glanced over and saw that Mr. Stanton had raised his camcorder again and was taping her. Josh saw her looking and waved.

"Oh no," Carole moaned. "He's getting up. I think he's going to come over here. What should I do?"

"I think you should do what C.C. would do," Stevie said helpfully. "Run."

Carole nodded. "I think I just might do that," she said. She was already feeling confused enough about all the male attention she was getting. The last thing she wanted to do was deal with more of it while she was trying to eat. "Did anyone happen to notice where the rest rooms are?"

"I did," Deborah told her. "They're right around the corner from the phone I was using. Past the check-in desk and down the hallway near the hotel bar."

"Thanks." Carole didn't wait around a second longer. She raced for the restaurant entrance, not pausing to see if Josh was trying to follow. He couldn't follow her into the women's room, at least.

She found the hallway and paused, taking a quick look over her shoulder. There was no sign of Josh.

"Good," she muttered. She didn't really have to use the rest room, so she leaned against the cool cement wall in the narrow hallway behind the phones and thought about what to do. If she went back in now, he would be waiting for her. She decided it would be best to hang out here for a while until the coast was clear. Luckily she had already eaten most of her dinner.

What is going on with these guys? she wondered. Back home, this kind of thing never happened to her. All three Joshes seemed perfectly nice, and all three were cute and interesting in their own ways. But why had all three suddenly decided that Carole was the girl of their dreams?

As she pondered the question, Carole gradually became aware of a familiar voice talking quietly and urgently nearby. She started to listen. It sounded like Garvey. He was talking on one of the pay phones just around the corner.

Carole was about to step forward and say hello to the trainer, but his next words froze her in place.

"You'd better not back out now," he said angrily, his voice getting a little louder, so that Carole could hear him more clearly. "You said you'd do it. And the race is tomorrow."

Carole frowned. Who could Garvey be talking to that way? She hoped it wasn't Toby. Garvey seemed to yell at the friendly jockey a lot.

"Ride her any way you want," Garvey continued, still sounding irate. "But when the right time comes, you'd better come through. Don't forget, it pays to be loyal to where you come from."

Maybe he *was* talking to Toby, Carole thought. Maybe he was telling Toby that he had better prove his loyalty to Maskee Farms by winning on Cookie Cutter the next day. But why would he call the jockey from a hotel to tell him that?

"Would you stop worrying so much?" Garvey snapped after a moment of silence. "I told you, you'll be well rewarded. And the stewards aren't going to suspect a thing. You've got a good record, right? They'll think it's just an accident."

Carole gulped. That didn't sound good. The stewards were the officials who watched every race and made sure the jockeys rode clean and fair. They had the power to change the official order of finish if they decided that one horse had interfered with another's performance or a jockey had done something improper or dangerous. She could hardly believe what she was hearing. Earlier, she and Lisa had made fun of Stevie for suspecting Garvey of something, but now it seemed she might really have stumbled onto another racetrack mystery.

She had to make sure it was really Garvey she was hearing. After all, a lot of people sounded alike, and she wouldn't want to accuse him unfairly.

Feeling proud of herself for thinking so rationally, she carefully peered around the corner. It was Garvey on the phone, all right. Unfortunately he was facing her way.

Carole drew her head back quickly, but it was too late. A second later she heard the phone clattering back onto its cradle. Before she could move a muscle, Garvey was in front of her, looking furious.

"Were you spying on me?" he roared, grabbing her arm. His giant hand covered her almost from shoulder to elbow, and his grip was so tight that it hurt.

"Let me go!" Carole cried, trying to twist away. "I didn't hear anything." She looked around desperately, but nobody else was in the hallway. And she hadn't seen anyone go into either of the rest rooms since she'd been standing there.

"You better not have," Garvey growled, leaning down to stare into her face. "And if you *did* hear anything you shouldn't have, you'd better forget it right away. Bad things happen to little girls who poke their noses into other people's business."

"Oh yeah?" Carole said, trying to sound braver than she felt. "Well, cheaters never prosper." It was something one of her teachers was always saying, and it had just popped into her head.

"What?" Garvey looked confused, and his grip loosened for a split second.

That was all the time Carole needed. She yanked her arm away and raced for the women's room. Once she was inside, she locked the door with trembling fingers.

"Hey!" Garvey pounded on the other side, sounding angrier than ever. "I know you're in there. Just listen up. Whatever you may think you heard, you're wrong. And don't you forget it." A second later there was the sound of heavy footsteps moving away.

CAROLE DIDN'T UNLOCK the door until she heard Stevie's voice calling her name outside.

"Thank goodness you're here!" Carole exclaimed, letting her in. "You'll never believe what just happened."

"You won't believe what happened to me, either," Stevie said. "I was just coming into that hallway outside to look for you, and guess who I ran into? Literally, I mean."

"Garvey," Carole said.

Stevie looked surprised. "How'd you guess?" she asked, leaning against the sink behind her. "He was in such a hurry I don't think he even recognized me. He certainly didn't stop to apologize for practically knocking me over." She rubbed her shoulder. "When a guy like that runs into you, believe me, you feel it."

Finally Stevie seemed to notice how upset Carole looked.

"Hey, what's the matter?" she said. "Don't tell me the other Joshes ganged up on you as you were crossing the lobby."

"Worse," Carole replied. She filled Stevie in on her encounter with Garvey.

Stevie's eyes widened. "Wow," she said. "It sounds like he was threatening you."

"It sounded that way to me, too," Carole said. "And just in case I forget it, the huge bruise on my upper arm will be there to remind me."

"I think it's time for a Saddle Club meeting," Stevie said. "We were all almost finished eating when you left, and Deborah has to go meet someone for her article now, so we ordered our desserts to go. Come on, let's go up to our room. If anything can help us figure out what to do about all this, it's double-chocolate mud cake."

"Sounds good to me," Carole said. She already felt better now that her friends were ready to help. Still, she couldn't help remembering the angry scowl on Garvey's face as he had yelled at her. She shivered a little as Stevie led the way to the lobby, where Lisa was waiting. Suddenly the three Joshes didn't seem like the worst of her problems.

"ARE YOU SURE he was talking to a jockey?" Lisa asked for the third time.

Carole licked some chocolate frosting off her plastic fork. The Saddle Club was sitting on one of the beds in their hotel room, polishing off their cake. "I'm pretty sure," Carole replied. "He told the person, 'Ride her any way you want to tomorrow,' or something like that. Who else could that be but a jockey?"

Stevie nodded. "I knew he was up to no good from the second I laid eyes on him," she declared.

"Well, I guess it's possible that you were right," Lisa admitted slowly. "There's only one question. What exactly *is* he up to?"

"I have no idea," Stevie said. "Maybe it's got something to do with gambling. Garvey could owe someone a huge amount of money and need to fix a race to pay off his debt. Or maybe the jockey he was talking to owes him money."

"I don't think so, Stevie," Lisa said, flicking a few crumbs off the bedspread. "Garvey told us he doesn't gamble, remember?"

Stevie shrugged. "Maybe he was lying."

"I doubt it," Carole put in. "Toby heard him say that, too, remember? He seems so honest that he probably would have said something if he knew Garvey was a big gambler."

"*If* he knew about it," Stevie argued.

But Carole had just had another thought. "Actually, now that I think about it, are we sure Toby is so honest? I hate to say it, but we don't know him that well. And if Garvey really was talking to a jockey, Toby would be the obvious suspect. He's riding both of the Maskee horses that are racing tomorrow." The bay colt was entered in a later race than the one in which Cookie Cutter was competing.

Lisa let out a sigh. "You know, the more we talk about this, the more I wonder if we're not way off base here," she said. "I mean, we already know that the racetrack has all kinds of terms and stuff that we don't know—like saying furlongs instead of yards or miles, and maiden races, and all sorts of other things. Isn't it possible—maybe even probable—that what Carole overheard was part of some totally innocent conversation?"

"But Garvey was so mad when he saw me," Carole protested, her hand automatically moving to rub her arm where the big man had grabbed it. It was still throbbing a little.

"He sure looked mad when I saw him," Stevie added helpfully.

Lisa shrugged. "So what? He got mad when Toby asked him a simple question about C.C.'s training. He was furious when he saw that we were younger than he was expecting. And he was practically fuming when Deborah mentioned his boxing career. Face it. The guy isn't exactly the most easygoing person in Kentucky. Maybe he was just angry because he thought you were eavesdropping."

Carole thought about her encounter with the trainer. "I suppose that's possible," she said slowly. "He does have an awfully quick temper. And he didn't really say anything that incriminating." She felt slightly relieved at Lisa's theory. Just because Garvey was gruff and easily annoyed didn't mean he was out to get her.

"But my hunch—" Stevie began.

"That's another thing," Lisa interrupted her. "I think we're just looking for mysteries because we found one the last time we were at a racetrack. But just because we're looking for one doesn't mean we're going to find one."

Carole almost smiled at that. When Lisa said "we," it was obvious she really meant "Stevie." And it was true. Stevie had been ready to distrust Garvey from the moment she met him. That wasn't fair—and it didn't make any more sense than the three Joshes falling all over themselves to talk to her. "I think you may have a point, Lisa."

"I think I do," Lisa said with a nod. "Garvey is a young, well-regarded trainer with everything going for him. That's why Deborah's putting him in her article, right? So why would he want to mess that up by doing something shady?"

Stevie looked ready to argue, but then she gave in and smiled. "Okay, okay," she said, swallowing her last bite of cake. "I still don't think it would hurt to keep an eye on Garvey, but maybe we should give him the benefit of the doubt. We're going to be busy enough tomorrow without any mysteries anyway."

"Good," Lisa said. "Then we're all agreed. Garvey's just a jerk with a bad temper. He isn't out to get us—at least, not any more than he's out to get the rest of the world. Right?"

"I guess so," Carole said. As she remembered Garvey's angry eyes peering into her own, she just hoped Lisa was right.

THE NEXT MORNING The Saddle Club was up early again. Deborah walked with the girls to the Maskee shed.

"I'll see you around post time, I hope," she said.

"Okay," Carole said, remembering that Deborah had to go back out to visit more farms that day. "I hope you make it. C.C. will be counting on having you there to cheer her on."

The girls greeted the horses and then helped the grooms with a few chores while they waited for Garvey to arrive. After her encounter with him the evening before, Carole was still feeling a little nervous about seeing the big man. But her friends had convinced her that he probably would have forgotten all about it by this morning.

Garvey arrived around six o'clock, just as the three girls stopped by Cookie Cutter's stall to feed her a few cabbage leaves. Toby was with the trainer. They were talking about the filly's chances in her race.

"I think if I can just keep her clear of the gray filly, she'll have no trouble with the others," Toby was saying.

"Don't worry about the gray," Garvey said. "You just steady her out of the gate like I said and give her some time to find her stride. If luck's on our side and you can manage to keep her out of traffic, there'll be no stopping her." He reached out, almost absentmindedly, and knocked on a wooden pillar. Carole almost smiled when she saw that. Josh A was right when he told her that people around here tended to be superstitious. Obviously, Garvey was no exception.

"I hear you, boss," Toby said. "I'll catch you later." He gave the girls a little wave and then hurried away.

Garvey glanced at them. "You three look like you need something to do," he said gruffly. "C.C. isn't working today since she's running this afternoon, but she could use a walk. You there." He pointed at Stevie. "Why don't you walk her down that path toward the parking lot and back. Give her something to look at other than the shed row. Don't let her graze too much along the way, though."

"Sure," Stevie said. She grabbed Cookie Cutter's halter and slipped it on the chestnut filly as Garvey looked at the other two girls.

"You." He pointed at Lisa this time. "Take the bay colt along with her. He's running today, too."

Lisa nodded and got to work. Carole glanced at Garvey but didn't meet his eyes. He was acting perfectly normal. If anything, he was being nicer to them than usual. But she still felt nervous. "Maybe I'll walk along with them in case they need help," she suggested, taking a step back toward Cookie Cutter, who was just emerging from her stall.

"Don't be ridiculous," the trainer snapped. "They'll be fine. There's too much work to do for you to start doubling up. I've got another job for you."

"Okay," Carole said weakly, watching out of the corner of her eye as Stevie and Lisa disappeared around the corner of the shed row with their charges. She suddenly felt very alone. Her friends were gone, Toby had left, and the grooms were nowhere in sight.

Garvey didn't seem to notice her consternation. "Your

friend the reporter tells me you're a good rider," he said. "Is that true? Because I've got a colt that could use some exercise, and my boys aren't here yet. Want to give him a try?"

Immediately all fearful thoughts fled from Carole's mind. She had ridden Prancer during her racing days, and it had been one of the most thrilling experiences of her life. She could hardly believe that Garvey was offering her the chance to do the same kind of thing. Obviously, whatever had happened the night before had been a huge misunderstanding. The trainer didn't seem angry at all now.

"I'd love to," she said eagerly.

"Good. Then come on." Garvey led the way to the last stall in the row. Inside was a colt named Storm Chaser. Carole had helped groom him the day before and knew he was frisky but friendly. Now she saw that he was already saddled and tied up in his stall, waiting.

"I asked the groom to tack him up," Garvey explained. He grabbed the colt's lead line and led him out of the shed row, with Carole following. Outside, the trainer turned in the opposite direction from the racetrack.

"Where are we going?" Carole asked, confused. "The track is the other way."

"I don't want to take him on the track today," Garvey replied without turning around. "One of his shoes is a little loose, and the dirt will only make it worse. There's a nice-

sized lawn behind the last barn where the horses graze sometimes. We'll just take him around that a few times."

Carole still felt confused. Like most racetracks, Bluegrass
Park had a grass racecourse, known as the turf course, inside
the main dirt track. Some horses specialized in running on
grass, some ran only on dirt, and some could go either way.
Carole wasn't sure why Storm Chaser would be able to exercise on a grassy lawn and not on the turf course. For a
second she thought about asking Garvey, but then she
thought better of it. He was being about as nice as he had
ever been since she had met him, and she was afraid the
wrong question could turn him mean and defensive again.
She didn't want to take any chances—especially when she
was about to take a ride on a real racehorse.

Making a mental note to ask her question later of someone friendlier, she followed Garvey as he led the colt toward
the lawn he had mentioned. Carole had passed it a couple of
times the day before and seen horses being grazed there, but
at this hour it was deserted. In fact, there was nobody in
sight at all, since the back of the nearest building blocked it
from view.

Garvey led Storm Chaser to a spot near the middle of the
lawn. He waited for Carole to catch up, then nodded
briskly. "Okay," he said. "I want you to get up there, then
trot him around the perimeter three or four times."

"But I should stop him if he's favoring the foot with the
loose shoe, right?" Carole asked. "Which foot is it, anyway?"

71

She hadn't noticed anything off about the colt's stride, but it was better to be safe than sorry.

"What?" Garvey said. "Oh, um, it's his left fore. Pull him up if he's having a problem."

"Okay," Carole said. She gazed up at the tall colt and smiled eagerly. "I'm ready."

Garvey unsnapped the horse's lead line and gave Carole a leg up. The ex-boxer was so big and strong that it was like being boosted by an elevator. The stirrups on the small saddle were higher than Carole was used to, so her right foot missed its mark as she settled into the saddle.

She never had a chance to make a second attempt at the stirrup. As soon as her rear touched the saddle, Storm Chaser let out a tremendous snort and bolted forward.

Taken by surprise, Carole grabbed a handful of the horse's mane in her left hand, trying desperately to regain her balance. She gripped the colt's sides tightly with both legs and scrabbled desperately for the reins with her right hand.

Storm Chaser came to an abrupt stop after only a few yards, but he wasn't finished. He whirled around and kicked up his heels in a quick buck and twist. By dropping the reins and grabbing his mane in both hands, Carole managed to stay aboard, though her left foot was jolted out of the stirrup. When the colt suddenly lowered his head and shook it violently, then whirled around and took off once again, Carole lost her seat and went flying off to one side.

She landed hard on the ground, the breath knocked out

of her. A quick glance showed her that Storm Chaser had stopped acting up as soon as she was off his back. Within seconds he was grazing peacefully nearby.

Carole soon determined that, luckily, she wouldn't suffer anything more than a sore rump as a result of her fall. As she got painfully to her feet, she saw Garvey walking calmly toward her, a small smile on his wide, ruddy face.

"What happened?" she gasped, doing her best to brush the dirt off her jeans.

Garvey stopped in front of her, his hands on his hips. "I'll tell you what happened," he said in a dangerously cool voice. "A little girl got herself into a situation she shouldn't have. And she almost got hurt. There are lots of ways to get yourself hurt around here. Gives you something to think about, doesn't it?"

Carole frowned, not understanding for a second. Then her eyes widened and she involuntarily stepped backward. Was Garvey threatening her?

He grinned at her expression. "I see we understand each other," he said. Then he turned and walked toward Storm Chaser, who was still grazing.

Carole gulped and watched him go. Could it be true? Had Garvey set this all up, knowing the colt would throw her, as a warning? It certainly seemed so. This had to mean that he was still angry about her unintentional eavesdropping the evening before. And *that* had to mean that he really was up to no good.

Before Carole could decide what to do next, Garvey returned with Storm Chaser. The colt stretched his head forward to nuzzle at her curiously.

"No hard feelings, right, boy?" she murmured, automatically reaching forward to pat the horse.

"That depends on what you do next," Garvey said, as if the comment had been directed at him. His eyes narrowed, and he took a step closer to Carole. "And whether you start blabbing about things you've heard—or *think* you've heard. Did you tell anybody about your spying last night? Anybody who might misunderstand—like that snoopy reporter pal of yours?"

Carole bit her lip and stared up at Garvey, mesmerized by the nasty look on his face. She was starting to feel really scared now. If the trainer would allow her to be thrown from a horse, what else would he be willing to do to shut her up if he thought it was necessary?

"Carole?" called a voice from nearby. "Hey, Carole. Is that you?"

Carole turned and almost laughed with relief as she saw Josh A heading across the lawn toward them.

Garvey let out an unintelligible growl, then abruptly turned and led Storm Chaser away. He didn't even acknowledge the boy as he hurried past, his strides so long that the leggy colt almost had to break into a trot to keep up.

Josh glanced over his shoulder at the horse as he reached Carole's side. "Wasn't that Storm Chaser?" he asked.

Carole nodded. Even now that the frightening moment

had passed, she didn't quite trust herself to speak. She never would have expected to be so glad to see one of the Joshes.

Josh looked at her, taking in her grass-stained jeans and mussed hair. "Hey, you weren't trying to ride him, were you?" he asked anxiously. "He's famous around here for dumping riders in the morning. I told you about him yesterday when I was telling you about Leprechaun's whip phobia, remember?"

"Oh." Carole thought back and remembered that Josh had mentioned a horse with that habit. "You did, I guess. But you didn't tell me his name."

"Really?" Josh said. "Sorry about that. But why would the trainer put you on him when he knew what would happen?"

Carole thought she knew the answer to that, but she didn't feel like sharing it with Josh. The last thing she wanted was to turn the boy into another target for Garvey's wrath. "I don't know," she said. "Come on, walk me back to the barn, okay?"

Immediately Josh seemed to forget all about Garvey and Storm Chaser. "Sure," he said eagerly.

As they walked, Josh chatted cheerfully about that afternoon's races and other topics. Carole did her best to answer appropriately and pretend to be interested in what he was saying, but her mind was elsewhere.

Garvey obviously wanted to make sure she didn't tell anyone about what she had overheard the previous evening. That left just one question: Exactly what *had* she overheard? Carole still had no idea what the trainer was up to, although this morning's events had convinced her that it had to be at least illicit, if not downright illegal. That meant she had to do something to try to stop him. But how could she do that if she didn't know what he was planning to do?

Carole sighed, then did her best to smile as Josh turned to give her another admiring look. It was time to call a Saddle Club meeting—and fast!

CAROLE MANAGED TO get rid of Josh by pretending that she was heading for the bathroom. As soon as he was out of sight, she turned and hurried to the Maskee shed row.

Peering inside, she saw that Stevie and Lisa had returned from their walk. They were in the process of cross-tying Cookie Cutter in the aisle. One of the grooms was at the other end of the row, grooming the bay colt.

Carole hurried over to her friends, glancing around cautiously for the trainer. "Hi," she said. "Where's Garvey?"

Lisa looked up. "Oh, there you are," she said. "We were just wondering what happened to you. Garvey just left with that horse Storm Chaser. He and Toby are taking him out to the track to work."

Carole winced at the mention of the colt's name. "I guess

he doesn't have a loose shoe after all," she muttered. "I should have known he wouldn't be working if he did."

"What?" Stevie glanced at her friend, puzzled, then reached into a grooming bucket for a hoof pick.

After checking to make sure the groom couldn't hear her, Carole quickly told her friends what had happened.

Lisa's eyes widened more and more with every word. "He actually said all that stuff?" she asked when Carole had finished.

Carole nodded. "Don't even try to tell me it's all a misunderstanding this time," she said. "Garvey all but came out and threatened me."

"Don't worry," Lisa said, switching the currycomb she was using to her other hand. "I'm convinced." She shook her head, looking angry. "I can't believe Garvey put you on that horse intentionally, knowing you'd be thrown. You could have been badly hurt!"

Stevie glanced at her friends across the filly's back. "And don't forget, he did it all in a totally out-of-the-way place," she said. "That way nobody would be likely to see and warn her."

"I know," Carole said. "I'm just lucky Josh happened along when he did, or who knows what might have happened."

"Josh?" Stevie said quickly. Carole hadn't mentioned his role in the story. "Which one?"

"Win," Carole said, blushing slightly. "I was just going to

78

mention him. He saw me and came running over, and that's when Garvey took off."

"I see," Lisa said, smiling a little. Then her face grew serious again. "You *are* lucky he came by. Garvey sounds dangerous. I think we need to talk to somebody about this right away. Like maybe the police or the track officials."

"I don't know about that." Carole had started combing out Cookie Cutter's silky mane while her friends worked on the filly's coat. Cookie Cutter was relaxed and seemed to be enjoying all the attention. "If you think about it, Garvey hasn't really said anything very specific. If we talked to someone official, it would be our word against his."

Stevie nodded. "And he's got a good reputation, remember? That's why Deborah's writing about him. Why would anyone believe us?"

"Especially when we don't even know what we're accusing him of," Lisa finished reluctantly. "I see what you mean. Still, we need to do something. Next time Carole might not be so lucky."

Stevie grinned. "I don't know about that. If all she needs is to have a Josh turn up to save the day, I'd say her odds are pretty good."

Carole stuck out her tongue at Stevie, then giggled in spite of herself. Talking to her friends was making her feel much better. If The Saddle Club worked on this problem as a team, they'd find a way to solve it. "Maybe we should talk to Deborah," she suggested.

Lisa's face brightened. "That's a great idea," she said. "She'll believe us. And she'll probably know what we should do next."

"Okay," Stevie said slowly. "I guess maybe we are in over our heads now." For Stevie, that was an unusual admission. Seeing her friends' surprised looks, she added, "Hey, I like a good mystery as much as anyone—maybe more—but not enough to put Carole in danger."

Carole nodded, her stomach tightening. "And Garvey's not stupid," she said. "He'll probably figure out that I've talked to you guys about this, if he hasn't already. Then we'll all be in danger."

"Come on," Lisa said, turning her attention back to her grooming. "Let's hurry up and finish with C.C. Then we'll go find Deborah."

THEY DIDN'T FIND Deborah in any of the nearby barns, so they headed for the track to see if she was there watching the workouts. She was nowhere in sight, but another familiar face was.

"Uh-oh," Stevie said under her breath, tugging at Carole's sleeve. "Mayday. Mayday. Josh alert at three o'clock."

But her warning came too late. Josh C, better known now as Show, had already seen them. He was standing near the rail with his parents. His father was taping a group of galloping horses with his camcorder. "Hey, Carole!" Josh called loudly. "Hi! Remember me?"

"How could I forget?" Carole said quietly with a groan.

But she did her best to smile as Josh came toward her. "Hi, Josh," she greeted him. "I don't think you met my friends yesterday." She quickly introduced Stevie and Lisa.

"Nice to meet you," Josh said politely. Then he grinned at Carole. "I bet you're surprised to see me here so early," he said proudly. "After talking to you last night, I convinced my parents to come watch the workouts this morning. They thought it was a really cool idea—you know, as part of the total Kentucky experience."

Carole glanced at her watch. It was about eight o'clock. She vaguely remembered telling Josh and his parents about the early-morning schedule at the track the evening before. It hadn't been easy to come up with things to talk to them about, even in the brief time she had spent taking their picture. Now she wished she had kept her mouth shut. She and her friends didn't have time to deal with a love-struck Josh right now. They had to find Deborah.

"That's nice," she said. "Um, I don't want to keep you from enjoying the action. So I guess I'll see you later." She started to turn away.

"Wait." Josh put a hand on her arm to stop her. Even after she stopped, he left his hand there, squeezing her wrist gently. "I thought maybe you could watch with me for a little while. You know, tell me what's going on and stuff." He shrugged and grinned again. "I hardly know anything at all about horses. Maybe you can teach me."

Stevie and Lisa exchanged glances. Normally there was nothing Carole liked more than talking to people about

81

horses. But this wasn't the time for one of her hourlong lectures.

"Sorry, Josh," Stevie said. "I'm sure Carole would love to help you out, but I'm afraid we've got to drag her away." She did her best to look apologetic. "She has a lot of work to do. She's taking care of the favorite for one of today's races." Noticing that Josh's father had turned and was taping them now, she added an elaborate shrug. "And unfortunately, work comes first."

"One of the favorites?" Josh said, looking impressed. "Wow! That's really cool. What's his name? I'll tell my dad to bet on him."

"It's a filly—um, a girl horse," Lisa said. "Her name is Cookie Cutter—Uh-oh."

Her friends turned to see what Lisa was looking at and gasped. It was Garvey. He had just appeared and was leaning on the rail, talking to an exercise boy, who was riding one of the Maskee horses.

"What's the matter?" Josh asked. He turned and stared in Garvey's direction, too, trying to see what the girls were looking at.

Stevie had an idea. "That's our boss over there in the blue shirt," she explained. "If he catches us here talking to you instead of working, he'll be really mad."

"Your boss?" Josh said. "Does that mean he owns Cookie Cutter?"

"He trains her," Lisa corrected.

"Wow!" Josh exclaimed. "That's really cool. Maybe you

could introduce me to him. I'd love to meet a real live horse trainer."

"I have a better idea," Stevie said. She turned and pointed to a large bay horse that had just stepped onto the racetrack. "See that horse over there? His name is . . . um . . . Pine Hollow. He's the fastest horse in all of Kentucky. You don't want to miss his workout."

"Really?" Josh's eyes widened as he watched the horse start to trot. "Wow. Thanks for the tip."

Stevie smiled. "You're welcome. Hurry, it looks like he's starting. You might want to get your father to tape him, too."

Josh nodded and raced over to his parents. Stevie watched long enough to see him grab his father by the arm and point toward the bay. Then she turned to her friends.

"Okay, let's make a break for it," she said. "Luckily, I don't think Garvey's noticed us yet."

As the three girls hurried back to the safety of the stable area, Lisa smiled at Stevie. "I wonder what that horse's name really is?" she said.

Stevie shrugged. "Who knows? But I think Pine Hollow is an awfully nice name for a racehorse, don't you?"

THE GIRLS STILL hadn't found Deborah a few minutes later when they met Toby leading one of the Maskee horses back from the track. Luckily, Garvey wasn't with him.

"Hi there," Toby said when he saw them. "What are you three up to?"

"We're looking for Deborah," Stevie said. "Have you seen her?"

The jockey shook his head. "Not lately. I thought she said something about visiting farms."

Lisa gasped. "That's right," she said. "She's going to be gone until post time, remember?"

"Is there a problem?" Toby asked, looking concerned. "Maybe I can help you out."

Carole shook her head quickly. "No, no problem," she assured him. "We just wanted to—um—find out what time we're leaving tonight. We can ask her later."

Toby nodded and continued on his way. Lisa watched him go. "Maybe we should tell him the truth," she whispered to her friends.

Carole shook her head again. "I don't think that's such a good idea," she said. "I'd like to trust Toby. But what if he was the one Garvey was talking to on the phone last night?"

"Good point," Stevie said. She glanced after the jockey. "Still, he seems so nice . . ."

"I know," Carole said. "But don't you remember, I told you Garvey said something about being loyal. Doesn't that sound like he was telling Toby he'd better win for Maskee Farms?"

"Maybe." Lisa frowned. "Besides, even if he's not involved in whatever it is, he might not believe us any more than the police would if we started accusing Garvey of being a crook."

"Or whatever," Carole added with a sigh. "That's the

worst thing. We don't even know what we're accusing him of."

"That's only part of the problem," Lisa said grimly. "We don't know, but Garvey thinks we do. That's why he wants to shut us up."

Carole glanced at her watch and gulped nervously. "And Deborah won't be back for hours."

"That settles it, then," Stevie said. "Until Deborah gets back this afternoon, we're just going to have to deal with Garvey ourselves."

8

THE GIRLS DECIDED to head out to the grandstand to talk, since Garvey wouldn't be likely to find them there. But someone else found them almost as soon as they made themselves comfortable on a bench.

"Carole!" Josh B exclaimed from behind them. "How are you?"

Carole fought back a groan of dismay as the older boy hurried over. Today he was wearing a clean white turtleneck and a pair of pressed black pants. "Hi, Josh," she said weakly.

"Hi, Josh," chorused Stevie and Lisa.

"Hi," Josh greeted them shortly. Then he turned all his attention back to Carole. "I'm really glad to see you again," he told her. "We didn't have nearly enough time to talk yesterday. I was hoping for a chance to show you around the track—you know, give you a taste of what I do here and how things work."

"That sounds awfully interesting," Carole said hesitantly. She didn't want to hurt the boy's feelings, but the last thing she needed right now was to be dragged off on some kind of grand tour of Bluegrass Park. How could she get out of it without being rude? For once, she wished she'd paid more attention when the girls at school or Pine Hollow were chattering on about how to talk to boys.

"But we really wouldn't want to take up so much of your time," Stevie continued—for her, smoothly—smiling innocently at Josh. "I'm sure your job keeps you really busy, right?"

"Well, yes," Josh said, glancing at Stevie as if trying to remember who she was. "It does. I have a lot of responsibility here, you know. My uncle really counts on me to keep things running."

"That's great," Lisa said. "You must be really good at what you do."

Josh smiled and straightened the collar of his turtleneck. "Well, I don't like to brag," he said. "But everyone says I'm a fast learner. I already know everything about how the front office runs, and I even know a little about the betting machines. As soon as I'm old enough, I'll probably start working at one of the windows."

Carole had seen the little windows where men and women sat behind the betting machines, punching in numbers and handing out tickets to the people who were gambling on the races. But she had never paid much attention to them, and she had given even less thought to the track's front office, whatever that was. She liked the track because horses were there. Everything else was just boring details.

She was sure Stevie and Lisa felt exactly the same way, but at the moment both of them were nodding and smiling at Josh as if his job were more exciting than a groom's, a jockey's, and the United States president's combined.

"Wow," Lisa said. "That's amazing. I feel bad even taking up this much of your time when you have so much to do."

Stevie stood up and grabbed Carole's arm. "Come on, Carole," she said, dragging her to her feet. "We'd better stop bothering Josh now and let him get back to work." She smiled at Josh again. "Maybe we'll see you later."

"Um, I hope so," Josh said, looking a little confused. "Bye, Carole."

The Saddle Club hurried away along the rail, leaving Josh staring after them. As soon as they were near the gap and safely out of sight, Stevie and Lisa broke into giggles. "That was fun," Stevie declared.

Lisa shrugged. "I don't know," she said with a smile. "I actually felt kind of sorry for him. He never knew what hit him."

Carole grinned at both of her friends. "Thanks, guys," she said gratefully. "You really helped me out back there. I couldn't think of a thing to say to him. If it was left to me, I'd probably be touring the snack bar or the program booth right now."

"You're welcome," Lisa answered for both of them. "But we shouldn't count on that working more than once. We'd better stick to less Josh-infested places for our meetings."

Carole's smile faded as she remembered the reason for their Saddle Club meeting. But before she could say a word, she heard a gruff voice behind them.

"Hey, you girls!" Garvey shouted. He had just rounded a corner and seen them.

"Oops," Stevie whispered. "Should we make a break for it? Those muscle-bound guys usually can't run very fast."

"Don't be ridiculous," Lisa hissed back. "He's not going to do anything to us here with all these people around."

Carole glanced around. At least two dozen people were nearby, from the jockeys on the track to the trainers watching them ride to a janitor sweeping up the grounds. That made her feel a little safer, but not much—especially when she got a good look at Garvey's glowering face.

"What are you three whispering about over here?" he demanded belligerently. The janitor looked up. Garvey noticed and lowered his voice. "I hope you're not telling secrets you shouldn't be telling."

"We don't know what you're talking about," Lisa spoke up bravely.

Garvey stared at her. "Oh yeah?" he growled. "I don't think I believe you. I know little girls tell their friends everything."

"You'd better watch out," Stevie said hotly, clenching her fists at her side. "We haven't told anybody what you're planning yet. But if you keep threatening us, we just might change our minds."

Garvey whirled to face her. "Threatening you?" he said. His angry face cracked into an ironic smile. "I'm not making any threats. Your imagination must be running away with you."

Lisa frowned, guessing what he was driving at. It was true that nothing he had said was concrete enough to be considered a threat if the girls told anyone. And now she knew that was no accident. She knew Deborah would believe them if they said Garvey was out to get them, but would anybody else?

"What about what you said to Carole about not blabbing to her reporter friend?" Stevie challenged him.

"What about it?" Garvey said, still smiling. "I was joking, that's all. You can't arrest me for having a different sense of humor than you do."

Meanwhile, Carole was gaping at the big man, astonished. "What about making me ride Storm Chaser when you knew I was going to get thrown!" she exclaimed. "Is that also your idea of a joke? A lot of people might not think it was funny."

Garvey shrugged. "That was an unfortunate accident," he said calmly. "Storm Chaser only throws his first rider of the day. After that he's safe enough for a five-year-old to handle. Toby told me he'd already ridden him today when he hadn't. Obviously."

It was clear that Garvey had thought this out. Lisa wondered if his excuse for putting Carole on Storm Chaser meant that Toby was in on the plot, too, as Carole suspected. Either way, Lisa knew that Garvey was lying. But they had no way of proving it. "What do you expect us to do now?" she asked the trainer.

Garvey shrugged again. "I don't expect a thing," he said. "Just for you girls to do the job you're getting paid for and mind your own business. What could be wrong with that?"

"Nothing," Stevie said. "But I should warn you: Anything that has to do with horses *is* our business."

Lisa groaned inwardly at Stevie's bold words. Garvey's face was getting red and thunderous again. His huge fists clenched and unclenched as if he wanted to strangle them all then and there.

But before he could respond, they all heard hoofbeats approaching the gap. It was Toby on one of the Maskee horses.

"He felt pretty relaxed out there," the jockey called out to Garvey, obviously not noticing the tension between him and the girls. "But he had a little trouble with his lead changes. He's not used to this wide of a curve, I guess."

"Don't tell me what my horses are used to," Garvey bellowed, whirling to face him. "I'm the trainer, not you. Got it? Now get that horse back to the barn and bring out the last one. We don't have all day."

Toby frowned, but he didn't speak in response to Garvey's

heated words. He just nodded and dismounted, leading the horse through the gap.

"You three, go with him," Garvey told the girls. "Someone needs to walk that animal and it's sure not going to be me." He lowered his voice a little so that Toby wouldn't hear. "And remember what we talked about, or we'll have to have another little discussion very soon."

The girls scurried to get away from Garvey and catch up with Toby. "Want me to lead him?" Stevie offered, reaching for the horse's lead line.

Toby nodded and let her take it. "Thanks," he muttered, shooting a glance back at Garvey, who had turned to watch the action on the track. "I wonder what that was all about?" He reached down and pulled a long, thin whip out of the side of his boot. As they walked, he tapped his hand with it rhythmically.

"I don't know," Lisa said. She wished they could tell the friendly jockey the truth, but they couldn't—not as long as they thought he might be in cahoots with Garvey. "He must have gotten up on the wrong side of the bed or something. I'm sure you were just trying to help."

"Thanks," Toby said, glancing at her gratefully. "It's nice to hear you say that. I only wish Garvey would realize it, too."

Carole was thinking about what the jockey had said. "What did you mean about the lead changes?" she asked. Being riders themselves, she and her friends knew all about lead changes, when a horse switched from beginning its stride with its left front leg to its right or vice versa. But Carole hadn't realized that racehorses needed to be able to change leads on command, and she said so.

Toby nodded. "That's a fair question," he said. "It's actually pretty logical. The lead foot takes a lot of pounding when a horse is running at full speed, so we like to make sure they change leads at least a couple of times during a race so one leg doesn't get more tired than the other. And since racehorses run counterclockwise around the track—in this country, at least—it makes sense for them to lead with their right leg during the two straight stretches on the course and switch to a left lead going around the turns."

"I get it," Stevie said. "That way their left leg sort of leads them around the curve."

"Right," Toby said. "Sometimes a jockey will have a horse switch leads when he's running down the homestretch, too. A fresh lead can give the horse an extra bit of energy when he's tired."

"That's really interesting," Carole said. "I'm surprised I never noticed the horses were doing that in the races I've seen."

"I'm surprised, too," Lisa said with a laugh. Seeing Toby's puzzled look, she added, "Usually Carole notices every single thing about every single horse she sees."

As Carole was starting to protest, another horse approached, led by a man even shorter and wirier than Toby.

He was leading a gray filly, and the girls immediately recognized Leprechaun. "Hey, Toby," the little man called. "Are you ready to lose in the second race this afternoon?"

Toby grinned. "Not on your life," he replied. He quickly introduced the girls to the other jockey, whose name was Mack.

Mack nodded a polite hello and then winked at them. "I beat Toby every time we run together," he said. "He just hasn't learned to admit it yet."

"Ha!" cried Toby, a twinkle in his eyes. "Don't listen to him, girls. I've left him in the dust the last ten or twenty times we've met. The only reason he's still getting mounts is that he's so small he never has any trouble making weight."

Carole smiled. She knew that each horse had an assigned weight to carry in a race, which included the weight of its jockey and tack. No trainer wanted his or her horse to carry more than the assigned amount, since it would slow the horse down, and that was why jockeys were so small and thin. Looking at the tiny Mack, Carole could imagine that no weight assignment could possibly be too low for him. In fact, he probably weighed no more than she did.

Mack grinned. "The day you beat me in a horse race, Toby, is the day I pack my bags and move straight back to Dry River," he said. "You might as well keep your filly in the barn this afternoon and save yourself the effort. Leprechaun will be crossing the finish line before you make it to the quarter pole."

Toby just laughed. "We'll see," he promised his friend.

"We'll just see about that, won't we, girl?" He reached over and gave Leprechaun a friendly slap on the neck. The filly snorted and eyed him suspiciously.

Mack said good-bye and continued on his way with the gray filly. Stevie turned to watch them go. "Do you think Leprechaun really might win today?" she asked Toby.

Toby shrugged. "Anything can happen on the track, and it usually does," he said. "But if racing luck is on our side, I think C.C. will take it in a walk."

As the group continued on its way, Carole had a different kind of question for the jockey. "I still don't quite understand how this distance thing works," she said. "Just now, Mack mentioned the quarter pole, and I know that's one of the poles around the track that measures the distance. But where is it exactly? And why is it there?"

"It can be a little confusing if you're not familiar with the system," Toby said. "The poles measure the distance around the track, but the trick to remember is that they count *backward* from the finish line. That means the quarter pole is a quarter of a mile—or two furlongs—before the finish if you're going counterclockwise. The three-eighths pole is one furlong, or an eighth of a mile, before that. And so on."

"I see," Carole said, and her friends nodded.

They were almost back to the shed row by now, but Toby paused for a moment to finish his explanation. "The poles are really useful for measuring distance when you're riding," he said. "When you see them go by, you know how much more of a race is left. And you can help your horse use his energy the best way so that he doesn't get overtired before the end." He glanced toward the row of stalls in front of them. "Could you take C.C. and cool her down?" he asked the girls. "I've got to go find one of the grooms to help me tack up the other horse."

"We can do better than that," Stevie said. "Lisa can walk C.C., and Carole and I will help you tack up."

"It's a deal," Toby said with a smile. "Let's go."

THE GIRLS DIDN'T see Garvey again for the rest of the morning. They walked Cookie Cutter and then pitched in to help the grooms with some other chores. They were so busy that they didn't have time to talk about Garvey's threats or anything else. By noon most of the work was finished and the girls' stomachs were grumbling.

"That should do it for now," one of the grooms said as Stevie swept the aisle. Carole and Lisa were putting the finishing touches on the tack that would be used in that afternoon's races. "You three are a big help—I wish you worked here all the time. Now go reward yourselves with some lunch, okay?"

The girls agreed quickly. "I'm famished," Lisa said as they left the shed row.

"Me too," Stevie said. "Should we head over to the grandstand and get something there? There's only an hour until post time."

96

Carole nodded. "That will give us just enough time for that Saddle Club meeting we've been trying to have."

"Right," Stevie replied. "We don't have much time if we're going to stop Garvey from carrying out his dastardly plan." She grinned ruefully. "Especially since we still have to figure out what it is."

9

LISA FOLLOWED HER friends as they walked between the rows of stables toward the gate leading to the public area of the track. Her mind had been nagging at her for a while now. She had the funniest feeling that they had missed a clue somewhere—maybe an important one that might tell them more about what Garvey was planning. What could it be?

"Come on, Lisa," Stevie said, pausing to glance at Lisa as she started to fall behind. "I'm dying for a huge, icy-cold soda. After all that hard work, my mouth is totally dry."

"That's it!" Lisa exclaimed, stopping short in the middle of the path. "That's the clue!"

"What?" Carole stopped, too.

"I knew that somebody had said something we should have noticed, but it just clicked," Lisa explained. "It was that other jockey, Mack. He said something about going home to Dry River. That's the name of the town Garvey is from, remember? He told Deborah that yesterday when she was interviewing him."

Stevie shrugged. "So they're from the same town," she said. "So what?"

"I don't know," Lisa admitted. "Maybe nothing. But it's kind of a funny coincidence, isn't it?"

"What are the odds of that, right?" Carole teased. "It *is* pretty weird. But I can't imagine what it could have to do with whatever's going on with Garvey."

"I don't, either," Lisa said. "But it's just about the only possible clue we have right now. And we need all the help we can get if we're going to figure this thing out."

"Carole! Hey, Carole! Wait up!" a voice called from farther down the path.

"Don't look now," Stevie whispered. "It's our good friend Win."

Carole glanced toward the voice out of the corner of her eye and saw Josh A heading their way. "Oh, no," she groaned. "I don't think I can face this right now."

"You don't have to," Stevie told her. "I have the perfect escape plan." She pointed across the path, and her friends turned and saw that they were standing right beside a set of public rest rooms.

"Perfect," Lisa said. "It's the one place none of the Joshes can follow us." The girls darted across the path and soon were safe inside the women's room. There was nobody else there at the moment.

Carole sat down on a metal bench near the door and sighed. "I seem to be spending a lot of time in the bathroom on this trip," she said, thinking of her escape from Garvey the night before.

Lisa shrugged and headed for one of the sinks. "At least this gives us a chance to wash our hands before we eat," she said.

"How long do you think it will take him to give up and go away?" Stevie asked, glancing at her watch. "My stomach won't wait much longer."

"Who knows?" Carole said. "I feel kind of bad for running away like that. He really is nice." She stood and joined Lisa at the sinks. "I just never know what to say when he starts showing off and acting weird. It's too bad in a way, because I like him fine when he's talking about horses."

Stevie nodded. "Some of the stuff he was telling us yesterday was pretty interesting," she said. "Like when he was talking about his job, and when he was talking about all the different habits and quirks that racehorses have."

Suddenly Lisa let out a gasp. "That's it!" she exclaimed.

Stevie cocked her head at her. "You've been saying that a lot lately," she said. "What is it this time?"

Lisa threw a balled-up paper towel at her. "Oh, nothing much," she said. "I've just solved the mystery, that's all."

"Really?" Carole grabbed her by the arm. "What is it?"

"First, tell me one more time what Garvey said on the

phone last night," Lisa said. "Try to remember the exact words."

Carole thought back carefully. "Let's see. The first thing I heard clearly was Garvey telling the person he was talking to not to back out, and saying the race was tomorrow—that's today."

Lisa nodded. "Then what?" she asked expectantly.

"Then he said, 'Ride her however you want,' or something like that." Carole could almost hear Garvey's gruff voice again as she remembered the phone conversation. "And he said that when the time was right the person had better come through. And that the person should be loyal to where he came from."

Carole gasped as she realized what she had just said. "That's it, isn't it?" she asked Lisa. "Where he came from, as in Dry River, Virginia."

"You mean he was talking to Mack?" Stevie asked with a puzzled frown. "I don't get it."

"Think about it," Lisa said. "They're both from the same place. And it sounds like that made Garvey think he could ask a favor."

"A *big* favor," Carole said. "The next part of their talk was about the stewards finding out, remember? What could it be?"

Lisa smiled and leaned back against the sinks, crossing her arms on her chest. "Isn't it obvious?" she said. She turned to Stevie. "It was what you said about horses' quirky habits that made me realize it. Josh told us that Leprechaun hates the whip, remember? So what better way to make sure she loses the race today than to convince her jockey to whip her?"

Stevie's mouth dropped open and she sat down on the bench. "That's so sneaky," she said. "But I guess it does fit our clues, doesn't it? And since Mack will be riding Leprechaun in a race for the first time, he could say he just forgot in the heat of the moment."

"It *is* sneaky," Carole said thoughtfully. "I've read about cases where jockeys have held their horses back on purpose and the stewards have caught them. But this is different. There's no way anyone could prove he did it on purpose. At worst, he'll probably get a warning."

Lisa nodded. "Leprechaun is C.C.'s only serious competition in that race. Everyone says so. Garvey obviously wants to do something to guarantee that his horse will win."

"But why?" Carole asked. "I mean, isn't he taking an awfully big chance? I'm sure that would be considered cheating. He could get in a lot of trouble."

"Money?" Stevie guessed, tapping her fingers on the bench next to her as she thought. "That always seems to be a good reason around here."

"I don't know," Lisa said slowly. "I guess that's a possibility. As trainer, I think he gets a percentage of whatever the horse wins, right?"

Carole nodded. "That's how it works," she confirmed. "But would the difference between the first- and second-place money be big enough to be worth it?"

"Probably not," Stevie said. "And we already know he doesn't gamble, so it's not that."

"What other reason could he have for wanting to win so badly?" Lisa mused.

Carole's empty stomach let out a sudden growl of protest, and she briefly wondered if Josh was still hanging around outside. Then she forgot about her hunger as an idea occurred to her. "What if he's doing it because he feels insecure?" she said.

Stevie gave her a skeptical look. "What?" she said. "I doubt that anyone would really—"

"No, wait. Listen," Carole interrupted. "Everyone at Maskee Farms is expecting C.C. to win this race, right? Maybe Garvey is afraid that everyone will blame him if she loses. He already had one career that was a big failure—he was a dud as a boxer. He might be trying to guarantee that his brilliant new career as a trainer doesn't end before it begins."

"But Mr. McLeod wouldn't fire him just because one horse lost a race it was supposed to win," Stevie said.

"*We* know that," Carole replied. "But Garvey must be feeling a lot of pressure since this is his first time in charge. He might not be thinking totally logically."

Lisa gave Carole an admiring glance. "Wow, that makes a lot of sense," she said. "How did you figure it out?"

Carole shrugged and smiled. "Let's just say I can relate to feeling a little insecure right now," she said, gesturing toward the door.

"Ah," Stevie said wisely. "The Joshes."

"The Joshes," Carole confirmed. "Every time one of them starts gazing at me like I'm the girl of his dreams, I feel like I'm suddenly supposed to be brilliant and amusing and everything else all rolled into one—you know, to live up to his expectations. So I can imagine how Garvey must feel, having such a promising horse being threatened with competition in her very first race—a race that he's been training her for."

Stevie nodded. "Especially since he hasn't been following the training schedule his boss gave him," she said, remembering Toby's comments. "Still, even if I were in Garvey's situation, I would never cheat my way out of it. That's just wrong. Besides, Leprechaun could get hurt if she panics when Mack whips her. Or cause an accident that hurts someone else."

"I know," Carole said. "That's why we've got to stop him. As much as I'd love to see C.C. win today, it won't mean anything unless she does it fairly. And I'm sure Mr. McLeod and the head trainer would feel exactly the same way."

"But what can we do?" Lisa asked.

The girls were silent for a moment. Finally Stevie looked at her watch. "Whatever we're going to do, we'd better do it soon," she said. "There's only a little over a half hour to post time now."

"Maybe we can find Mack and talk to him," Carole said, standing up. "It sounded like Garvey was having trouble convincing him to go along with his plan. We might be able to change his mind."

Lisa shrugged. "I can't think of anything better to try." She shuddered. "We definitely shouldn't waste our time trying to talk to Garvey. But how are we going to find Mack?"

"Let's check the jockeys' room," Stevie suggested. "Maybe he's there already, getting ready for the race."

The girls headed for the rest room door. As soon as they emerged into the sunlight, they saw that Josh A was leaning against the wall beside the door.

He straightened up when he saw them. "Hi!" he said brightly. "I saw you go in there. I guess you didn't hear me calling you." He smiled at Carole. "So I decided to wait for you out here."

Stevie rolled her eyes. They had been inside the women's room for fifteen or twenty minutes. She couldn't believe that Josh had waited for them—or rather, for Carole—all that time. But since he was here, she decided they might as well take advantage of it. "Listen, Josh," she said. "Do you have any idea where we could find Leprechaun's jockey? We really need to talk to him."

Josh looked surprised. "Mack?" he said. "As a matter of fact, I do know where he probably is right now."

"Where?" Lisa asked breathlessly. "In the jockeys' room?"

"Nope. Every race day here at Bluegrass he has lunch at the same hot dog stand." Josh gestured toward the grandstand. "It's a little out-of-the-way place just past the lost and found. He always gets the same thing—a chili dog with all the trimmings and a cup of coffee. It's sort of a superstitious thing he does for luck." He grinned. "He's the only jockey I know who could get away with that kind of habit and still make weight. In fact—"

Stevie cut him off before he could finish. "Thanks for the info," she said quickly. "We'll see you around, okay?"

"I can show you where the snack bar is if you want," Josh volunteered eagerly, taking a step closer to Carole. "And actually, I was looking for you because I have some great news I wanted to tell you about. I just found out that I get to lead Leprechaun to the paddock all by myself. And if she wins, I get to—"

Once again, Stevie interrupted before he could finish. "That's great, Josh, but we've really got to go." She dragged Carole away before the boy could say another word.

Carole glanced back at Josh over her shoulder as the three girls hurried away toward the entrance to the grandstand. He was staring after them, looking dejected and a little hurt. "You could at least have let him finish his sentence," Carole told Stevie, feeling bad about being so rude. "He seemed really excited about his news."

"We don't have time for that right now," Stevie replied, speeding up a little. "We've got a race to save."

Lisa gave Carole a sympathetic glance. "Don't worry," she advised. "The best thing you can do for Josh right now is to give Leprechaun a fair chance. Otherwise there's no way he'll get to take her anywhere near the winner's circle."

"I guess you're right," Carole said reluctantly. She still felt guilty, but there was nothing she could do about it right now. Maybe later she could find Josh and apologize.

As soon as The Saddle Club entered the grandstand, they found another obstacle looming in front of them. It was Josh B, also known as Place.

"I was hoping to run into you," he said, rushing over to Carole. "I have some time to give you a tour of the track now if you're still interested. I might even be able to introduce you to my uncle if he's not too busy. I told him all about you."

Carole blushed furiously at that, but Stevie and Lisa were already brushing past the tall boy. "Sorry, no time right now," Stevie said briskly. "We've got an important errand to run."

"Oh, really?" Josh said. "Maybe I can help. I know this place like the back of my—"

"Thanks, but no thanks," Stevie said.

Lisa shot him an apologetic glance. "Sorry," she added, pulling Carole forward.

The girls dove into the crowd that was starting to gather in the main concourse of the grandstand. Carole paused just long enough to peek back at Josh. The expression on his face was almost identical to the one the first Josh had been wearing just a moment earlier. Once again Carole felt bad. Still, she hadn't asked the boys to like her. She couldn't help it if their feelings were hurt now.

Stevie paused in front of an ice-cream cart and looked

around. "Let's see," she said. "He said it was near the lost and found, right?" She asked the woman scooping out ice cream for directions, and soon they were on their way, dodging around track visitors.

"At least it isn't as crowded as it was at the Preakness," Lisa panted, jumping aside to avoid tripping over a toddler.

"Thank goodness!" Stevie exclaimed. Suddenly she let out a groan of dismay. "Oh, no," she said. "When it rains, it pours."

Carole glanced forward and saw that Josh C was standing in front of them, taping them with his father's camcorder as they approached.

"Hi there," he called, lowering the camera. "I can't wait for the racing to start, can you? It's going to be totally awesome."

The girls had reached him by this time. "Sure, Josh," Stevie said quickly. "Whatever you say."

She went past him, and Carole started to follow. But Josh reached out to stop her. "Hey, wait a second," he said. "Where are you going? I was just about to invite you to come sit in the clubhouse with me. All three of you, I mean," he said, turning away from Carole long enough to give the other two girls a brief smile. "My parents reserved a box of seats. That way, maybe you can help me with my taping." He waved the camcorder. "My dad's letting me use this for the whole afternoon. Isn't that cool?"

Carole opened her mouth to answer, but Lisa didn't give her a chance. "Sorry, Josh," she said, smiling politely.

"Maybe later." She yanked on Carole's arm, pulling her past the astonished-looking boy.

"I really feel bad about this," Carole said as she jogged alongside her friends in the direction the ice-cream vendor had sent them. "We're being so rude."

"Desperate times, desperate measures and all that," Stevie said firmly. "You can deal with the Joshes later if you want." She tossed a glance toward Carole. "Anyway, since when do you *want* to hang around talking to the Joshes? Usually you can't get away fast enough."

Carole just shrugged. She couldn't explain it herself. But she knew her abrupt departures were making the boys unhappy. And she couldn't help feeling responsible for that, even if she hadn't asked for their attention in the first place.

Just then Lisa pointed at a sign ahead. "There's the lost and found. We're almost there."

The crowd thinned out as they continued past the lost and found kiosk and around the corner beyond. When they reached the snack bar, which was set back off the main area, there was hardly anybody around at all. That made it easy for the girls to spot Mack. He was standing in front of the snack bar with a newspaper tucked under one arm. Garvey was standing right next to him.

Carole gasped and jumped back behind a large pillar, out of the men's sight. Her friends did the same thing.

"What's he doing here?" Lisa whispered.

Stevie nodded grimly toward the two men. "Look."

The snack bar attendant had his back to the men at the

counter as he prepared a hot dog. Garvey had just pulled a long white envelope out of his pocket. He gave a quick glance around, but luckily he didn't see the girls. After checking to make sure the attendant still wasn't looking, he shoved the envelope toward Mack.

The jockey accepted the package and turned his back to the counter. Then he lifted the flap of the envelope and pulled it open a little bit. Even from where they were standing, the girls clearly saw a flash of green inside before Mack closed the flap and tucked the envelope into his pocket.

"Money," Stevie whispered. "Garvey's paying him off."

"He said he'd be rewarded," Carole recalled, thinking back to the phone conversation once again. "I guess he meant that literally."

"And here we thought he was doing it out of hometown loyalty," Lisa said, ducking back farther as Garvey hurried past the pillar on his way out of the snack area. "Talking him out of the plan might not be as easy as we thought now."

THE SADDLE CLUB waited behind the pillar for a moment more to make sure Garvey was gone for good. They watched as the jockey reached out to take the dripping chili dog that the counterperson handed him, along with a steaming cup of coffee. Mack carried his food over to one of the small round tables nearby. Unfolding his newspaper, which the girls could now see was the *Daily Racing Form*, he settled down to his lunch.

"Okay, let's go," Stevie whispered. She led the way toward the jockey's table.

It took him a moment to notice them. Finally he looked up from his paper, squinting as if trying to recall where he'd seen them before.

"Hi, Mack," Stevie said, pulling out a chair and sitting down across from him. "Remember us?"

The jockey looked nervous for a moment. Then his expression cleared. "Oh, you're those girls who were helping Toby, right?" he said. He watched warily as Carole and Lisa sat down on either side of Stevie. "What are you doing here?"

"We just want to talk to you for a minute," Carole said. "We were curious about something."

"Yes?" Mack still looked suspicious and a little worried.

Carole glanced at her friends for support. Stevie smiled encouragingly. "We heard something about a horse you're riding today," Carole said. "Leprechaun. We heard she has an unusual phobia about being whipped, and we were wondering if it was true."

Mack looked more nervous than ever. But he just shrugged. "That's what they tell me," he said. "I've never raced her before, so I couldn't tell you for sure." He took a big bite of his chili dog.

Stevie decided it was time for her to take over the questioning. Carole was being a little too subtle, and they didn't have much time. "Look," she said, leaning forward on her elbows so that her face was close to the little man's. "We know all about what Garvey's trying to pull today. And we saw him give you that money, so we know you're planning to go along with him."

Mack swallowed his food and raised the chili dog for another bite. "I don't know what you're talking about," he muttered.

"Please," Lisa said. "We don't need you to confess or anything. We just want you to think about what you're doing. Don't you care about making it a fair race? Don't you want Leprechaun to have the chance to do her best? She could be hurt, you know—or worse. And she could hurt the other horses and riders in the race."

The jockey frowned, and for a second his eyes seemed sad. Then the expression vanished and his face was a complete blank. Staring at the girls, he slowly picked up his chili dog and shoved the rest of it into his mouth. Then he grabbed his newspaper, stood up, and hurried away.

Stevie stood as if to follow, but Lisa stopped her. "Forget it," she said dejectedly. "We did what we could. If he's still determined to cheat, there's nothing else we can do to stop him."

"Sure there is," Stevie said heatedly. "We could go to the stewards and tell them what we know. Maybe they can make Garvey confess, or get Mack to turn in his whip before he rides—"

"I don't think so," Carole broke in. "The stewards aren't going to believe us. It's a pretty wild story, if you think about it. I can hardly believe it myself. Besides, there's not enough time. The first race will be starting any minute." She sighed. "We'll just have to cross our fingers and hope that Mack thinks about what we said and decides to do the right thing."

Lisa crossed her fingers and smiled. "Does this make us superstitious racetrackers?" she asked, holding up her hand.

113

"I don't know," Stevie said. She crossed her fingers, too. "But we need all the luck we can get—racing or otherwise. Come on, let's grab some food and go watch the race."

A FEW MINUTES later the girls were at the grandstand rail gobbling down hot dogs and sodas. The post parade had just started, but they hardly saw the horses prancing by in front of them as they continued to talk about Garvey and Mack.

"Maybe our little talk will scare him out of doing it," Stevie said hopefully, licking mustard off her fingers. "He might be afraid we'll go to the stewards with what we know after the race. They'd have to listen to us then, wouldn't they?"

"Maybe," Lisa said, looking doubtful. "But if he and Garvey both deny the whole thing, what can they do? There's no evidence."

"What about the money?" Carole asked.

Lisa shrugged. "Garvey may be crooked, but he's not stupid," she said. "He paid Mack in cash, remember? And I don't think there was any writing on the envelope. I doubt there's any way to trace that money back to him."

Just then something made Carole turn around and glance behind her. Josh A was standing a few yards away, and she was pretty sure he had been looking at her. But as soon as she turned, he whirled around and hurried away. Carole frowned, feeling worse than ever about brushing him off earlier.

"I think I've lost one of my admirers," she said, telling her friends what she had just seen.

Stevie shrugged. "One down and two to go." She gave Carole a close look. "Unless you've actually started to like one of them, that is," she added.

"No, not really," Carole said. "I mean, I don't know any of them well enough to know whether I like them." She sighed. "But that doesn't mean I want them to hate me, either."

They all stopped talking and watched the horses finish warming up and then take their places in the starting gate. With a clang of the starter's bell, they were off.

For a moment, the girls were caught up in the excitement of the race. They cheered as a speedy little roan colt battled for the lead with a rangy bay. But by the time the roan was posing for his picture in the winner's circle, The Saddle Club's attention had turned to the next race.

"Should we go down to the paddock and watch C.C. get saddled?" Carole asked.

Lisa shuddered. "No way," she said. "Don't forget who's doing the saddling."

"Oh yeah." Carole had forgotten that trainers accompanied their horses to the paddock. "Let's stay here."

"I have a better idea," Stevie said. "Let's look for Deborah."

Lisa's expression brightened. "You know, I almost forgot about her. She should be back by now," she said. "Maybe there's still time to stop Mack before the race."

The girls split up so they could search a larger area. But when they met again at the same spot by the rail fifteen minutes later, none of them had found her.

"Maybe she got held up at one of the farms," Lisa said, leaning on the rail dejectedly.

Carole nodded. "Or she might be down in the paddock with Garvey and the other trainers."

At that moment the horses were called onto the track for the second race. The girls turned and watched as the horses started stepping through the gap.

"The moment of truth," Stevie muttered, watching for Cookie Cutter.

The chestnut filly was fourth in line, three spaces ahead of Leprechaun. Like the rest of the jockeys, Toby and Mack were now dressed in colorful silks.

"Did you know that jockeys' silks really used to be made of silk?" Carole commented aimlessly. "Now they're mostly nylon, I think."

Her friends didn't bother to answer.

Lisa rested her chin on her arm, watching the horses walk past the grandstand and then turn and head for the starting gate on the far side of the track. Some trotted to warm up, others cantered or galloped. Cookie Cutter seemed to be frisky and ready to run. So did Leprechaun. Would they both have a chance to do their best? Lisa hoped so. She crossed her fingers again, then glanced at her friends. Both of them had their fingers crossed on both hands.

Stevie took her eyes off the horses long enough to squint

at the huge tote board in the middle of the track, trying to figure out what the information on it meant. "Look," she said. "C.C. and Leprechaun have the same odds. I think."

Lisa looked, too. "I think you're right," she said. The number four was posted beside each of the fillies' numbers. "I think that means their odds are four to one, right? So people must think they both have a good chance to win."

Carole just shrugged. She wasn't interested in the odds. All she was interested in was a safe and fair race. "What if Leprechaun bolts when he hits her and runs into other horses?" she commented worriedly. "That could cause a bad accident, especially if she's in the lead when she does it."

Stevie didn't hear her. She was too busy eavesdropping on a young couple standing nearby. "Did you hear that?" she whispered. "That woman just bet ten dollars on Leprechaun to place." That meant the woman would collect money if Leprechaun came in first or second in the race.

"I hope she wins that bet," Lisa said grimly.

Soon the horses started entering the starting gate. They looked small and distant across the expanse of the infield, but The Saddle Club could recognize Cookie Cutter easily by her bright chestnut coat and Toby's colorful silks.

Lisa gripped the rail, feeling the excitement of race time wash over her despite her worry. This was Cookie Cutter's big debut, and she looked ready for it. The filly stepped daintily into the metal starting box, and a moment later all the other horses were in, too. Lisa held her breath and waited for the starter's bell.

"And they're off!" the announcer cried a second later as the horses broke from the gate as a group, pounding forward down the track. It took a moment for Lisa to locate Cookie Cutter among the other horses, but then she saw her. She was near the middle of the pack, right next to Leprechaun.

For the first few furlongs they both stayed right there. Lisa kept her eyes on the chestnut filly, not bothering to pay attention to the three horses that were trading the lead back and forth at the front.

Just as the horses reached the beginning of the wide turn, Cookie Cutter started to move up. She passed one horse after another, and at the middle of the turn she dove between two other horses to take the lead. "Look! Look!" Lisa squealed, jumping up and down. "She's winning!"

"Here comes Leprechaun," Stevie shouted, pointing.

Lisa took her eyes off Cookie Cutter and saw that the gray filly had also pulled ahead of the other horses to challenge her rival.

"Hey, they both did lead changes right there," Carole commented as the two fillies swept out of the turn and started down the homestretch.

Lisa hardly heard her. She was cheering loudly as Cookie Cutter bravely held off Leprechaun's challenge for several strides. But Leprechaun kept coming, and after a moment she began to gain on the chestnut. A few more strides, and she was a nose in front, and then a full head.

Her heart in her throat, Lisa watched Mack, who was no more than a blur of silks crouched on the horse's back. The time had come. If he was going to throw the race by whipping Leprechaun, this was the time to do it. There were less than two furlongs to go until the finish line.

The next few seconds seemed to pass very slowly indeed, at least to The Saddle Club. Without looking at each other, each girl knew that the others were holding their breath and crossing their fingers.

Finally, as Cookie Cutter battled back to within a nose of her competitor, Mack made his move. But he didn't reach for his whip. Instead, he started rocking back and forth, his hands seeming to push the horse's head forward with every stride.

Lisa heard Carole gasp beside her. "He's hand-riding her," she exclaimed. "He's not going for the whip. He's trying to win!"

All three girls started cheering loudly. At first Lisa wasn't sure if she was cheering for the sweating, straining horses on the track or for the jockey who had decided to do what was right. But by the time the finish line loomed, she was definitely cheering for Cookie Cutter. Stride by stride, the chestnut filly was regaining the ground she had lost to Leprechaun. Soon they were neck and neck. Then Cookie Cutter pulled ahead once again. By the time the two flashed under the wire, the brave chestnut was almost half a length in front. Leprechaun was second, more than three lengths in front of the rest of the field.

"She won!" the three girls cried in one voice. They hugged each other gleefully, then let out another loud cheer. It felt very good, and Lisa knew why. Cookie Cutter had won the race fair and square.

"THAT WAS GREAT," Carole said as they watched Cookie Cutter walk back along the track toward the winner's circle. But her friends noticed she wasn't smiling anymore.

"What's wrong?" Lisa asked.

Carole sighed. "It's great that Mack decided not to help Garvey cheat," she said. "But it means we really have no way of proving that Garvey did anything wrong. And that means he might do something rotten another time—and get away with it."

Stevie pointed toward the winner's circle. "Speak of the devil," she said.

The others looked and saw that Garvey was standing near the winner's circle, waiting for Cookie Cutter. He was smiling, but even at this distance Stevie thought his expression looked rather forced. "Even though C.C. won the race, I bet

121

he's seething because Mack didn't do what he wanted," she said.

Lisa nodded, but Carole didn't respond. She was staring down the rail. "Carole?" Stevie said. She turned to see what her friend was looking at and saw Josh A waiting for Leprechaun at the gap. "Oh."

"I guess he gets to lead her back for unsaddling, too," Carole said. She sighed. "I still feel bad about cutting him off before when he was so excited."

"I feel worse about letting Garvey get away with what he did—or what he tried to do, that is," Stevie said, returning her attention to the winner's circle. There had to be something they could do to prove what Garvey was really like. One option was to find Deborah, tell her everything, and hope that she could help them convince the stewards or Mr. McLeod that the assistant trainer was up to no good. But that plan seemed a little too chancy for Stevie's taste. She was sure she could come up with something better if she just put her mind to it . . .

She watched thoughtfully as Garvey led the chestnut filly inside and held her head while a photographer snapped a picture. Then Toby dismounted, he and Garvey shook hands with a few well-wishers, and it was over. A groom stepped forward to lead the tired filly back to the barn for some well-earned rest.

"Should we go back and see if they need us to cool her down?" Carole asked.

Stevie shook her head firmly. "They'll manage without us," she said. "We have more important things to do."

Lisa and Carole turned to give her a questioning look. They recognized that tone of voice. Stevie was up to something.

Stevie saw the look on their faces and grinned. "You didn't think I was just going to sit back and let him get away with it, did you?" she asked. "We've got to come up with a plan. Maybe we can trick him somehow—you know, trap him into admitting the whole thing. That worked last time, remember?" Their last mystery at the racetrack had ended when The Saddle Club had managed to trick the culprit into confessing.

"I don't know," Lisa said. "We got really lucky last time. That's the only reason it worked then." She shrugged. "This time I have the feeling the only one who's ever going to hear anything about this again is Mack, as soon as Garvey tracks him down."

Stevie shuddered. She had seen the burly assistant trainer get angry, but she had the feeling that what she had seen was nothing compared to what Mack was going to see. She would hate to be in the jockey's shoes right now.

Carole, too, was thinking about what Lisa had just said. And she was starting to get an idea about what they could do. It was risky, but it just might work. "I've got it," she said excitedly. "I know what we can do!"

"What?" Stevie demanded.

Carole shook her head and hurried away in the direction of the clubhouse. "I'll tell you as we go," she called back. "We're going to need some help, and we don't have much time."

Stevie and Lisa exchanged looks and shrugged. Then they set off after their friend.

MOMENTS LATER, THE three girls were racing toward the unsaddling area. "I just hope we aren't too late," Carole panted. It had taken her a little longer than she had hoped to find Josh C, who was now running along with them, his father's camcorder in his hand.

"Is anyone going to tell me what this is all about?" he asked plaintively, glancing from one girl to another.

"No time right now," Carole said. She had outlined the basics of her plan to Stevie and Lisa during their search for Josh, but that was different. Her best friends knew the whole story and had caught on quickly. Josh wasn't likely to understand without hearing the entire story in full detail, and she didn't want him backing out now. They needed him for the plan to work. "Sorry. Just trust me, okay?"

"Sure," Josh said with an adoring smile, speeding up a little so that he was running closer to her.

When they reached the unsaddling area, Carole thought for a moment that they were too late. Most of the fillies from the second race had already left for their individual barns. But then she spotted a familiar gray tail swishing across the ring. It was Leprechaun. Josh A was holding her bridle and talking to an older man.

"There she is," Lisa gasped. "But where's Mack?"

"There's only one way to find out," Stevie said.

She charged across the ring and confronted Josh. He blinked at her in surprise. "What are you doing here?" he asked.

Stevie didn't bother to answer the question. "Where's Mack?" she barked.

Josh's confused look changed to one of annoyance. "What do I look like, his baby-sitter?" he said.

Stevie clenched her fists and opened her mouth to answer. But Carole, who had joined them by this time, shoved her aside. "Sorry about that, Josh," she said, much more calmly than she felt. "We don't mean to be rude, but we're kind of anxious to talk to Mack, and since you were so much help when we were looking for him before, we figured you were the most likely person to know where we could find him now. Could you help us out? Please?" She smiled widely at him and blinked her eyes a few times as she'd seen actresses do on TV. She felt a little silly doing it, but it seemed to work. Josh still looked suspicious, but he tentatively returned her smile.

"Um, well, okay," he said slowly. He had just noticed Josh C standing behind Carole, and he frowned. But he went on. "He already weighed out and headed back to the jockeys' room to change."

"Thanks, Josh," Carole told him sincerely, giving him another big smile. Stevie and Lisa had already taken off in the direction of the jockeys' room, Josh C in tow. But Carole paused for another moment. "We really do appreciate it," she told the boy. "And I promise to explain everything later, okay?"

"Okay." This time Josh's smile was a lot bigger. "Oh, by the way, Mack is riding again in the fourth race, so he'll probably be in the jockeys' room for a few more minutes," he offered.

"Thanks." Carole paused for one last grateful smile, then took off after her friends.

"THIS SHOULD DO," Stevie muttered, pushing aside some branches of the thick bushes flanking the door to the jockeys' room. "After you, Show—er, I mean, Josh," she said, holding the branches back to reveal a hollow space near the center of the bush. "There should be just enough room for all of us."

Josh stared at Stevie, then glanced down at his clean khaki shorts and white T-shirt. "Um . . . ," he began.

"I'll go first," Carole volunteered, stepping forward. She ducked down and crawled into the hiding place. "Very cozy," she pronounced, sitting down on the dirt.

That was all Josh needed to hear. A moment later he was seated next to her, so close that their knees touched. "This is cool," he said, grinning at her and leaning a little closer.

"We're coming in," Stevie announced. She crawled in beside the pair, and Lisa followed. Soon all four of them were crouched in the tiny hiding space in the hedge.

"Wow. Talk about togetherness," Lisa said, moving her arm to avoid a scratchy branch.

Stevie elbowed Josh in the ribs. "Can you see out at all from where you're sitting?" she asked. "You're going to need to be able to tape what's going on outside."

Josh wiggled around a little until he was able to poke the camcorder through a bare spot. He peered through the viewfinder. "I can see a little bit," he said dubiously. "I just hope whatever or whoever you want me to tape is going to be standing right in front of us, though, or you're out of luck."

Stevie frowned, but Carole wasn't worried. "It doesn't matter," she said. "Even if we can't get a good picture, we should be able to pick up the sound track we need. That's more important anyway."

"Really?" Josh sat back and tapped the top of the camcorder. "That's good. This thing has an awesome microphone. It picks up everything."

"Heads up!" Lisa hissed. She was peering through the branches. "Someone's coming."

They all looked out. "It's Garvey," Stevie whispered, recognizing the big man easily, even though she could only see him from the elbows down. "Your plan's working perfectly so far, Carole."

Carole smiled and held one finger to her lips as Josh gave her a questioning look. She pointed to the camera, and he

127

obediently went into his taping position. "Switch it on when I tap you on the arm," she whispered in his ear.

"Keep your fingers crossed," Lisa murmured to her friends.

They waited for what felt like forever. Josh had to shift position slightly once or twice to stay comfortable. The three girls sat completely still, watching Garvey, who was visible in patches through the shrubbery as he paced back and forth.

Finally they all heard the sound of the jockeys' room door slamming shut. "This could be it," Stevie whispered.

"Shhh!" Carole leaned forward a little, trying to see who had come out. Before she could get a good look, she heard Garvey stomp forward.

"I've got a few things to discuss with you, little man," he growled.

Her heart in her throat, Carole tapped Josh on the elbow. He obediently switched on the camcorder and leaned forward a little farther, trying to get Garvey in view.

Next Mack's voice came toward them clearly. "I don't want to hear it, Garvey," the jockey said brusquely.

"Well, you're going to hear it," Garvey replied. Suddenly the two men moved to a spot where Carole could see them clearly through a break in the leaves. Garvey had taken hold of the smaller man's arm and was dragging him straight toward their hiding place!

"Uh-oh," she muttered. A moment later they all ducked back as the branches around them bent back under Mack's weight. Garvey had just shoved him into the hedge.

128

"Watch it," the jockey said calmly. "I've got to ride in these silks."

Garvey didn't answer. "Come here," he said, his voice getting quieter as he moved away. "We've got to talk in private."

Carole's heart sank. If Garvey dragged Mack off to an empty stall in one of the shed rows or the men's room or someplace else, the plan would be ruined. They hadn't taped him saying anything incriminating yet.

Luckily Mack didn't seem eager to go anywhere with the big trainer. "If you've got something to say, say it right here," he said belligerently, his voice still close and clear.

Garvey let out an indecipherable grumble. "At least come over here behind these bushes," he said at last. "The whole track doesn't need to hear this." Apparently the jockey nodded agreement, because the next sound the girls heard was footsteps moving around the side of the hedge where they were hiding.

Lisa gasped and scooted forward. "Do you think they'll be able to see us?" she whispered frantically. The branches in the back of the hedge were thinner than those in front.

Carole gulped and turned around. The last thing she wanted was for Garvey to catch them spying on him. "Just keep as far back as you can," she said helplessly, shrinking away from the sound of the footsteps.

"And think green," Stevie added in a whisper. The men's legs were clearly visible to all four of the hiders as they emerged and stopped about two yards in front of them. By crouching farther down and looking up, the girls could see their angry faces.

Josh hadn't missed a beat. The camera was still running, and he leaned forward just a little to get a clear shot of the two men. Carole bit her lip and watched him, hoping that his white shirt wasn't too obvious among the green branches.

Luckily, the men didn't even glance in their direction. They were standing on the bare patch of dirt between the hedge and the outside wall of the jockeys' room, glaring at each other.

"Now," Garvey said slowly. "Would you care to explain yourself?"

Mack shrugged. "What's to explain?" he said. "Anyway, what do you care? Your horse won anyway, didn't she?"

"That's not the point!" Garvey shouted. Then, remembering where he was, he lowered his voice. "I paid you to do a job, and you didn't do it. Doesn't your word mean anything, you lousy cheat?"

"You're the cheater, not me," the jockey replied. "You're just lucky I'm not going to talk to the track officials."

Garvey balled one hand into a fist and punched it into his other hand. "You'd better not turn me in, little man," he said, his voice dangerously low.

"Save your threats," Mack said, sounding annoyed. "I'm not interested. And if you have any intention of pulling something like this again, leave me out of it. I never felt right about it in the first place. Leprechaun is a good filly, and she deserves her chance. I only listened because I thought I owed it to you, since we grew up together."

"You owe me more than a listen now, that's for sure." Garvey took a step closer.

The jockey reached back and pulled something out of the waistband of his fitted white nylon pants. It was a long white envelope. "Don't worry, I wasn't going to keep your stinking money," he said. "Here. I'm sure you'll need it to pay someone else to do your dirty work."

Carole forgot her nervousness and grinned. Turning, she saw that Stevie and Lisa looked just as thrilled. Garvey, with Mack's help, was confessing to everything—and he didn't even know it! Glancing at Josh, she saw that he looked puzzled, as if trying to figure out what was going on. Promising herself to fill him in fully when it was all over, Carole turned her attention back to the men.

Garvey snatched the envelope, opened it, and pulled out the bills inside. After counting the money, he nodded and stuffed it into his pocket. "I should whip you for not whipping that filly," he said. "You could have cost me everything. And you're a fool, man. That money was a lot more than your ten percent would've been even if your horse had won."

Mack just shrugged. "Not everybody is a slave to money, Garvey," he said, turning away from the big man to go back around the hedge. He paused and glanced back. "Actually, it was some folks from your own barn who helped me realize it. You could take some lessons on sportsmanship from them."

Garvey grabbed the jockey by the shoulder. "What's that supposed to mean?" he bellowed. "You better not have told anybody about our little arrangement, or you'll be very, very sorry. Was it that rat Toby?"

Mack didn't reply. He just twisted out of Garvey's grip and turned to face him. "It wasn't Toby. Now leave me alone. I've said all I have to say to you, you oversized jerk."

That was more than Garvey could stand. He swung a huge fist toward the jockey's face.

The girls gasped in horror. But Mack was too quick for Garvey. He ducked the punch easily, then took a few steps out of range. Grinning, he shook his head. "No wonder you never made it as a boxer," he said. Then he was gone.

With a roar of frustrated rage, Garvey pounded his fist into his own thigh. "It had to be Toby," he muttered to himself. "I'll pound him into—Wait." He paused. "He said 'them.' Could it be . . . ?" A look of amazement crossed his face, followed by one of rage.

He didn't bother to go around the bushes the way he had come. Instead, he shoved his way right through the hedge. His heavily booted foot missed Lisa's leg by inches, but he never looked down and didn't see The Saddle Club and Josh cowering in their hiding place.

Carole was still shaking minutes after the trainer had disappeared. "Wow," she said at last, her voice quavering.

"That was close." She glanced at Josh. "You can turn off the camera now."

"Oh!" The boy seemed a little surprised. He glanced at the camcorder, which had fallen into his lap after the big man's departure. He flipped the Off switch. "Who *was* that guy, anyway?" Apparently he hadn't recognized Garvey from when the girls had pointed him out that morning. But Carole didn't want to take the time to fill him in right then.

"I'll explain everything in a little while," she said, grabbing Josh's hand and squeezing it. "Okay? Right now we need to take that tape and show it to someone."

"Okay." Josh glanced down at their joined hands and smiled.

Carole gulped and let go of his hand. She hadn't even been aware of what she was doing. Somehow, in the last few minutes, she had stopped thinking of Josh as a guy who liked her and started thinking of him as just another co-conspirator. But now most of her embarrassment flooded back in full force. Still, this time she was determined not to hurt anyone's feelings.

"Um, all right then," she said. She held out her hand, and Josh popped the tape out of the camcorder and handed it to her. "Thanks, Josh. We'll—I'll come find you in your parents' box in a few minutes. I promise."

Josh nodded and crawled out of the hiding place. The three girls followed. With a quick wave, they left him and set off toward the shed row.

"I really hope Deborah is back by now," Lisa muttered as they jogged along the path.

Carole hadn't thought of the possibility that Deborah hadn't yet returned from her trip into the country. "If she's not, maybe we can give the tape to an official for safekeeping," she said. "Or maybe Toby will help us."

"Or maybe we'll just have to hide in the bathroom until Deborah gets back," Stevie suggested with a grin. "Hey, I just realized something. This will give Deborah another really big scoop to write about, won't it?"

Lisa nodded, but she wasn't really thinking about Deborah's reporting career at the moment. "At least we shouldn't have to worry about running into Garvey," she pointed out. "That bay colt is in the fourth race. Garvey's probably already in the paddock with him."

Lisa was in the lead as the trio rounded the corner into the shed row, so she was the one who actually ran smack into Garvey, who was standing just inside the doorway. Stevie ran into Lisa, and Carole stopped just short of colliding with Stevie. She clutched the tape tightly and looked up at the towering trainer.

"Uh-oh," she said.

Garvey seemed a little surprised at their abrupt arrival, but he didn't waste any time. He grabbed Lisa's arm in one hand and reached for Stevie with the other. "Just the little girls I was looking for," he growled.

Carole backed away a few steps and cast a desperate look

around. The Maskee shed row was deserted, and the bay colt's stall door was standing open. She guessed that the rest of the staff had gone to the paddock for the fourth race. That meant that The Saddle Club was alone with Garvey.

"Let them go," Carole said. She was hoping to sound brave, and was embarrassed to find that her voice came out in a high squeak.

Stevie and Lisa were twisting and wiggling, but they couldn't break Garvey's grasp. "Come here," Garvey said menacingly, staring at Carole.

Carole took another step backward and stuck the tape behind her back. "Why should I?" she challenged him.

Garvey caught the motion and his eyes narrowed. "What's that you have?" he said. "A videotape?" He was silent for a second, his mind working that one over. As he realized what it might mean, his frown grew deeper still.

"Run, Carole!" Stevie shouted. "He doesn't dare do anything to us—ouch!" she yelped, as Garvey's grip tightened on her upper arm.

Carole hesitated, not sure what to do. Would the trainer hurt her friends if she left them and ran for help? Or would he let them go and chase her? She didn't like the sound of either option.

Before she could decide what to do, Garvey started dragging her struggling friends farther into the building. Carole took a tentative step after him. "Where are you going?"

Garvey gave her a nasty smile. "I'm moving this discussion to someplace more private." He continued down the aisle, pulling Stevie and Lisa as easily as if they were bales of hay, despite their best efforts to hook their feet around pillars and drag their heels on the dirt floor. A moment later he had dragged them into the tack room, which was really just a large box stall.

Carole hurried to the doorway and peered in. "Carole, no!" Lisa cried. But it was too late. Garvey's arm darted out and yanked her inside. When she caught her breath, Carole saw that Garvey had let Lisa go. She was cowering in the corner, while Stevie continued to squirm in Garvey's other hand.

Suddenly Lisa darted forward, trying to get past Carole and out of the stall. But Garvey moved so that his huge bulk blocked the doorway. Carole managed to jerk free, but she and Lisa were both still trapped inside the makeshift tack room. Stevie, who was still trapped in Garvey's steely grip, finally stopped her efforts to escape and stood still.

"There, that's better," Garvey said with satisfaction, surveying his three captives. "Now maybe we can have a reasonable discussion about this little situation. What do you say?"

There was a long moment of silence as the girls stared at him, then turned to look at each other. What would happen now? Carole felt the bulky videotape she still clutched in her hand. If she gave it to him, would he let them go? Or would he keep them here and try to make them promise not to tell anyone what they knew? Maybe they could convince him somehow that this was all a big misunderstanding. If he thought they didn't know anything about the payoff, they might still get away free.

"Well?" Garvey said at last, letting go of Stevie and crossing his arms on his massive chest. "I'm waiting."

One look at his expression convinced Carole that it would be useless to pretend at this point. He knew they were onto him.

"Yo!" yelled a familiar youthful voice from just behind the trainer.

Garvey looked surprised, then turned slowly to face the newcomer. The girls could see Josh C standing just outside the doorway, his hands on his hips.

"Josh!" Carole cried in amazement and fear. He must have followed them. Now he would be in just as much trouble as the rest of them.

At that moment, Josh A stepped forward, taking his place at Josh C's side.

"Josh!" Lisa exclaimed.

Next, Josh B came into view on Josh C's other side.

"Josh!" Stevie said. "I mean, Joshes!"

Garvey scowled at the three boys. "What's this all about?" he said. "Who are you kids, and what do you want?"

"We're here to make sure you don't hurt our friends," Josh A spoke up bravely.

"Oh yeah?" Garvey put his hands on his hips and surveyed his challengers. A small smile played around the corner of his lips. "Do you really think you three puny little boys can stop me?"

Carole wasn't sure about that at all, and she hated the thought that the Joshes might get hurt because of her. She briefly wondered how and why they had teamed up, but there was no time to think about that now. She had to stop this before it went any further.

"Garvey, just listen to us for a minute," she pleaded. "We all know what you did." That wasn't strictly true, since as far as she knew the three boys were still in the dark about the whole scheme. But she plowed on. "If you'll just turn yourself in and promise never to do it again, I'm sure Mr. McLeod will forgive you."

Garvey laughed humorlessly. "Don't be an idiot," he hissed. "Nobody's ever going to know about this except you kids. And I'm going to give you a little hint right now about what might happen if you decide to blab to anyone about it." He grabbed Josh A by the collar of his shirt and dragged him forward. He drew back one huge fist and then paused. "Which do you like better, your stomach or your nose?" he growled.

"He likes them both, and you'd better not touch either one," called an authoritative voice from just behind the boys. As Garvey dropped his fist in surprise, a man The Saddle Club had never seen before stepped into view. He was wearing slacks and a sports jacket, and a horseshoe-patterned tie was knotted loosely around his neck.

138

"Wh-Wha—" Garvey sputtered, but before he could complete the thought, two more people joined the man.

"Deborah!" Lisa cried out in relief.

"And Toby!" Stevie exclaimed when she saw the jockey.

"What's going on here?" Deborah demanded. She hurried forward and shoved her way past Garvey, who stepped aside to let her past, looking stunned. "Was he threatening you, girls?" she asked, putting one arm around Lisa and the other around Carole.

"He sure was," said Josh A, giving Garvey an angry glance. He straightened his lucky T-shirt where the trainer had grabbed it. "Until we showed up, that is."

Carole almost laughed at the boy's defiant words. Even if you put all three Joshes together, they would still have only half Garvey's strength.

"I see," Deborah said. But she still looked confused.

"I can explain it all, Uncle Lou," said Josh B, turning to the man in the tie.

Stevie gasped. "You're Josh's uncle?" she asked. "The track manager?"

The man nodded. "That's right, young lady," he said. He gave Garvey a suspicious glance. "And we're going to get to the bottom of whatever's going on here, don't you worry. Why don't we all move to my office?"

"There's really no need for—" Garvey began.

"Quiet," Uncle Lou snapped in a no-nonsense voice. "We'll discuss it in my office."

Garvey gave The Saddle Club one last murderous glance

139

before meekly turning to follow the track manager. Toby, looking very confused about what was going on, had to excuse himself to hurry to the paddock for the fourth race. But he promised to join them as soon as it was over.

"I wonder why Uncle Lou turned up just in the nick of time?" Stevie asked as the girls and the Joshes followed the adults down the shed row.

Josh B turned and grinned at her proudly. "I called him," he said. "When I ran into these guys in the grandstand"— he gestured to the other two Joshes—"we all compared notes and realized something strange was going on. We thought you might need some help, so I asked Uncle Lou to meet us here."

"Unfortunately, he was a little late," Josh A said ruefully. "I was afraid we were all going to be flattened to a pulp before he got here."

Josh C flexed his muscles. "I wasn't scared at all," he declared. But when Carole gave him a dubious glance, he grinned. "Well, hardly at all," he amended.

"I can't believe it," Lisa said. "You mean you three guys recognized each other and decided to get together and help us?"

"Sure," Josh A said with a shrug. "I can always recognize my competition, whether it's a horse or . . ." He let his voice drift off, but The Saddle Club knew exactly what he meant. He had seen both the other Joshes and recognized that both were also interested in Carole.

"Right," Josh C continued. "At first our little chat wasn't

exactly . . . um . . . polite, but as soon as we all realized you girls might be in trouble, we decided we'd better try to find out what was going on."

"Wow," Carole said.

Josh B turned to her and smiled. "Now we have just one question for you," he said. "What *was* going on?"

At that, The Saddle Club laughed so hard that Deborah and Uncle Lou turned to look at them. Garvey glared at the three girls, but Uncle Lou's hand on his arm reminded the trainer to keep his mouth shut. Finally Carole got control of her giggles. "I think you'll find out in just a minute when we get to your uncle's office," she told Josh B. "If anything is still unclear after that, we'll explain everything, okay?"

"Okay," Josh B said, and the other two boys nodded agreeably.

They soon reached the grandstand, and Uncle Lou led the way inside, turning down a corridor the girls hadn't noticed before. Offices lined both sides.

Josh A had looked thoughtful as they walked. Now he turned to Carole. "Whatever was happening back there, it looked like you were lucky we turned up when we did," he said somberly.

Carole nodded. That was true. Even if the boys couldn't have held Garvey off for very long, their arrival had surprised the trainer enough to buy them a few very crucial moments. Otherwise, he might have grabbed the tape and made his escape before the other adults turned up. "It was very lucky," she told him.

"And you know what that's called, don't you?" Stevie said.

The boys looked confused, but Carole and Lisa knew exactly what she meant. The Saddle Club grinned. Then, in one voice, the girls exclaimed, "Racing luck!"

12

STEVIE YAWNED BROADLY. "I can't believe Deborah still has the energy to drive after such a long day," she murmured, closing her eyes.

Lisa nodded. "I know what you mean. But she misses her baby," she reminded Stevie. "I guess that gives her extra energy."

"Food is supposed to give you energy, too," Stevie said, opening one eye for a moment. "But all that food we just had made me awfully sleepy."

It was early evening. The girls and Deborah had just finished dinner. Josh B's uncle had insisted on taking the whole group out and charging the meal to his expense account. He said it was his way of apologizing on behalf of the entire racetrack for what had happened. Naturally, Garvey was not invited.

Lisa glanced out the car window toward the hotel office. She could see Deborah inside, waiting in line to check out. "I was already tired by the time we got to the restaurant," Lisa admitted, smothering a yawn of her own. "The only thing that kept me awake was watching the Joshes fight over sitting next to Carole."

Carole blushed. "That was pretty embarrassing," she said. "I'm just glad you guys were there to save me." After watching the shuffling for a few minutes, Stevie and Lisa had decided to come to the rescue. They had taken Carole's arms and planted her firmly in a chair between the two of them. The boys had had to be content with gazing at her from across the table.

Stevie sat up and opened her eyes again, grinning as she remembered the scene. "For a while there, those guys looked more like The Three Stooges than the good old Win, Place, and Show that we know and love," she said.

"Don't forget, we don't know where we'd be right now without them," Carole said. "They really did save the day, in a way."

Stevie raised an eyebrow at her. "Oh?" she teased. "Coming to their defense, huh? Does this mean you're starting to return their affections?" She winked at Lisa. "Just think how jealous all the girls back home will be when they hear Carole has *three* boyfriends."

Lisa giggled, and Carole couldn't help joining in. "Seriously, though," Carole said a moment later. "I appreciate everything they did—and I let them know it, too." She had taken a few minutes after dinner to pull each boy aside and thank him for his part in the plan. "But still, I can't help being relieved that they all live so far away. I'm not sure I could take that kind of attention full-time."

Lisa nodded sympathetically. "I understand," she said. "But this won't be the last time something like this happens, you know." She smiled at Carole fondly. "A whole lot of boys are going to fall head over heels for you, and you'd better get used to that idea."

"I'm trying," Carole said. "But it's not easy." Suddenly she thought of the perfect way to explain to her friends how she felt. "Nobody who knew what they were doing would pick out a horse as soon as they laid eyes on it, would they?" she said. "They'd have to look it over more closely, get to know it a little, have a vet examine it. So why would a boy just pick out a girl at first sight?"

Stevie laughed. "Would you prefer they called their vets to check you out first?" she teased.

Carole smiled. "Well, you know what I mean."

"Of course we do." Lisa reached over to give her a hug. "And don't worry. No matter how strange all the boys around you may act, you can count on us to help you through it."

"Thanks," Carole said gratefully, hugging Lisa back.

"Does this mean the Joshes are totally out of the picture?" Stevie asked. "Too bad. They were starting to grow on me."

"Well, actually . . . ," Carole began slowly.

Stevie and Lisa turned to look at her. "What?" Stevie

demanded. "They're *not* out of the picture? You didn't get engaged to two or three of them and not tell us, did you?"

Carole rolled her eyes and laughed. "Hardly," she said. "But I did exchange addresses with one of them."

"Really? Which one?" Lisa asked.

"I know," Stevie said. "Josh A. Am I right?"

Carole nodded. "He was the only one I thought I had something in common with."

"Of course," Lisa said, smacking herself on the forehead. "I should have realized you'd go for the one who spends all his time with horses."

"That's not all," Carole went on. "I also started to like him better when we talked after dinner. He admitted that the first thing he liked about me was that I seemed to know something about the racetrack—he had overheard me talking about C.C.'s legs, remember? So he didn't just like me for the way I look." She blushed again. "Although he said he liked that, too," she added in a murmur.

Stevie and Lisa exchanged grins. "I guess you picked the right name for him, Stevie," Lisa said. "Win was the winner after all."

Carole stuck out her tongue at her. "Very funny," she said. "I didn't say he's my boyfriend now or anything. We're just going to write to each other—you know, about horses and stuff. After all, he lives in Kentucky." She shrugged. "Anyway, I don't think I'm ready to have a boyfriend right now."

Stevie and Lisa nodded. They understood perfectly. For

now, Carole was still more interested in horses than in boys. They all knew that might change someday, but for now it was just fine.

"Anyway," Stevie said, settling back against the seat once again, "Joshes or no Joshes, this turned out to be a pretty interesting weekend, didn't it?"

"It sure did." Lisa looked back out the window at the office. Deborah was still in line, but now there was only one person ahead of her. "What do you think Garvey will do now?"

"Who cares?" Carole said. "The important thing is that he won't have the chance to endanger any more racehorses with his crazy schemes."

That afternoon, after he had heard the girls' story and seen their tape, the track manager had called Mack and the track stewards to his office. Leprechaun's jockey had confessed to everything as soon as he realized what was happening. The stewards had suspended his jockey's license for a month and barred Garvey from the track permanently. That meant the big man's career as a trainer was essentially over, since all other tracks would honor the ban as well. At first he had started blustering at the girls and the room in general, tossing out all kinds of threats. But a few stern words from the head steward had humbled him, and he had remained silent while Deborah called Mr. McLeod and gave him the news.

The girls' theory turned out to be correct: Garvey admitted that he had been so afraid of looking bad if Cookie

Cutter lost that he had tried to guarantee that she would win. He was afraid that otherwise his career as a trainer would fizzle before it began, just like his boxing career, and he couldn't stand to go through that humiliation again. The other adults in the room had seemed surprised at the ex-boxer's motive, but the girls had already figured out that not every bad deed could be traced directly to money—not even in a money-driven business like horse racing.

"I was really worried that the rest of the Maskee horses weren't going to be able to run in their races next week after Mr. McLeod fired Garvey," Stevie commented. Without a trainer at Bluegrass Park to supervise them, Mr. McLeod would have had no choice but to send the horses home.

"Me too," Carole agreed. "Who would have guessed that Toby had just earned his trainer's license?"

"*We* should have." Lisa yawned again. "That must be why he was so concerned about Garvey's changing the training schedule. He knew Garvey might be messing up his horses' chances."

"Luckily the horses are better at their jobs than Garvey was," Stevie pointed out. Not only had Cookie Cutter won the second race, but the bay colt had placed a close second in the fourth.

"That is lucky," Carole said. "And Toby was lucky to be in the right place at the right time." Mr. McLeod had immediately appointed the jockey, who had joined the others in the office by then, acting assistant trainer for Maskee Farms,

effective immediately, with the strong possibility of a full-
time positon once the owner and head trainer returned from
California. Toby had accepted on the spot, even though it
had meant canceling a few rides he'd had lined up with
other trainers for the coming week.

"He seemed really happy," Lisa said. "He said he's always
wanted to be a trainer, and now he'll have his chance."

"I'm sure he'll do great," Stevie said, snuggling against the
car door, trying to find a comfortable position.

Just then Deborah returned from the office and climbed
into the driver's seat. "All set," she announced. "Ready to
go?"

"We're ready," Lisa replied.

Deborah started the car and pulled out of the hotel parking lot. Soon they were tooling down the highway, heading
east, away from the setting sun.

The motion of the car was making Stevie sleepier than
ever, but she fought to keep her eyes open. There was still so
much to talk about. "Can you believe that we've solved two
mysteries in the two times we've been to the track?"

Deborah glanced at her in the rearview mirror. "I sure
can't believe it," she said, shaking her head. "Even for you
three, that's a pretty amazing streak."

"It is pretty weird," Carole said. "I guess there must be
more mysterious things happening at the racetrack than
most places."

"I don't think so," Deborah replied. "I've spent quite a bit of time at the track lately, working on stories, and the only times anything odd happened there were when you girls were with me."

"Maybe we're just better at uncovering the strange stuff than most people," Stevie suggested.

Deborah signaled and smoothly changed lanes before answering. "I don't think that's it," she said. "Despite what some people think, the racetrack doesn't really have any more scandals and funny business than anyplace else. I think there's something else at work here. Something very strange."

"What are you saying?" Lisa asked, blinking sleepily at the scenery rolling by outside.

Deborah grinned. "I'm saying that you three attract adventure like a magnet," she declared. "Who else but The Saddle Club could have so many wild and wonderful things happen to them?"

Lisa shrugged. She hadn't thought of it that way, but she had to admit it was true. The three friends had definitely had more than their share of adventure—and fun. "I guess we're just lucky."

"I guess so," Deborah said. "And I must say, it's a really interesting kind of luck."

"Racing luck?" Carole said.

"It's better than that," Stevie said with a grin. "It's Saddle Club luck. We have it, and nobody else in the world does."

Lisa smiled at her two best friends. "Right. And what are the odds of that?"

ABOUT THE AUTHOR

BONNIE BRYANT is the author of many books for young readers, including novelizations of movie hits such as *Teenage Mutant Ninja Turtles* and *Honey, I Blew Up the Kid*, written under her married name, B. B. Hiller.

Ms. Bryant began writing The Saddle Club in 1986. Although she had done some riding before that, she intensified her studies then and found herself learning right along with her characters Stevie, Carole, and Lisa. She claims that they are all much better riders than she is.

Ms. Bryant was born and raised in New York City. She still lives there, in Greenwich Village, with her two sons.

Don't miss Bonnie Bryant's next exciting Saddle Club adventure . . .

NIGHTMARE
Saddle Club Super Edition #6

When a fatal equine virus breaks out at a nearby stable, The Saddle Club has to endure forty-five days of waiting and worrying about whether the disease will reach Pine Hollow. Then Carole realizes that one of her favorite horses may already be infected, and she decides to take matters into her own hands and hide the horse. Can Carole protect Pine Hollow? Or will she discover that there is nothing she can do to keep her worst nightmare from becoming reality?

Meanwhile, Lisa is trying not to let her competitive urges rule her life. So what if a classmate wants to be valedictorian? So what if graduation is still eight long months away? She doesn't always have to be the best, does she? Will the classroom become Lisa's worst nightmare?

Stevie has found a mysterious place in the woods. Is she on the trail of an Underground Railroad route? Or is she chasing after nothing? And what really happened here? Was it a journey to freedom? Or someone's worst nightmare come true?